"Hudsons don't hide."

"Well, maybe pregnant ones should."

They were squaring off in his living room. Him all sooty and sweaty, and her, perfectly fine, except for the rising tide of nausea she was desperately trying to ignore.

And worse, so much worse, the little wiggle of softness at the idea that he wanted to protect her. Even as she convinced herself he only wanted to protect the current *vessel* of his child, she felt that warmth.

You are a fool, Anna Hudson.

A fool who usually preferred a fight. To wear down her opponent until she got her way. Because she always won. Always got her way.

She had the very frightening thought that Hawk might not wear down as easily.

COLD CASE INVESTIGATION

NICOLE HELM

H HARLEQUIN

INTRIGUE

For all the heroes I've denied.

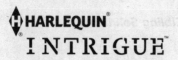

INTRIGUE™

Recycling programs
for this product may
not exist in your area.

ISBN-13: 978-1-335-59163-0

Cold Case Investigation

Copyright © 2024 by Nicole Helm

All rights reserved. No part of this book may be used or reproduced in any manner whatsoever without written permission except in the case of brief quotations embodied in critical articles and reviews.

This is a work of fiction. Names, characters, places and incidents are either the product of the author's imagination or are used fictitiously. Any resemblance to actual persons, living or dead, businesses, companies, events or locales is entirely coincidental.

For questions and comments about the quality of this book, please contact us at CustomerService@Harlequin.com.

TM and ® are trademarks of Harlequin Enterprises ULC.

Harlequin Enterprises ULC
22 Adelaide St. West, 41st Floor
Toronto, Ontario M5H 4E3, Canada
www.Harlequin.com

Printed in Lithuania

MIX
Paper | Supporting
responsible forestry
FSC® C021394

Nicole Helm grew up with her nose in a book and the dream of one day becoming a writer. Luckily, after a few failed career choices, she gets to follow that dream—writing down-to-earth contemporary romance and romantic suspense. From farmers to cowboys, Midwest to *the* West, Nicole writes stories about people finding themselves and finding love in the process. She lives in Missouri with her husband and two sons, and dreams of someday owning a barn.

Books by Nicole Helm

Harlequin Intrigue

Hudson Sibling Solutions

Cold Case Kidnapping
Cold Case Identity
Cold Case Investigation

Covert Cowboy Soldiers

The Lost Hart Triplet
Small Town Vanishing
One Night Standoff
Shot in the Dark
Casing the Copycat
Clandestine Baby

A North Star Novel Series

Summer Stalker
Shot Through the Heart
Mountainside Murder
Cowboy in the Crosshairs
Dodging Bullets in Blue Valley
Undercover Rescue

Visit the Author Profile page at Harlequin.com.

CAST OF CHARACTERS

Anna Hudson—The youngest Hudson sibling and a private investigator who also works with her siblings at Hudson Sibling Solutions as an investigator.

Hawk Steele—Bent County fire inspector who is investigating the fire that was meant to kill Anna.

Jack Hudson—Eldest Hudson sibling, sheriff of Sunrise, Wyoming, and head of Hudson Sibling Solutions.

Palmer Hudson—Anna's closest brother and an investigator at HSS.

Louisa O'Brien—Anna's best friend from childhood who is dating Palmer.

Mary Hudson—Anna's only sister and the administrative assistant of HSS.

Cash Hudson—Anna's brother who works as a dog trainer for his own company that sometimes helps HSS with search dogs, etc.

Izzy Hudson—Cash's eleven-year-old daughter and Anna's niece.

Grant Hudson—Anna's brother, former military and current HSS investigator who is dating Dahlia Easton.

Chapter One

Anna Hudson was no stranger to mistakes. She was an act first, think later type of person. Because more often than not, that worked out for her.

And if she was being bracingly honest with herself—which her current situation seemed to call for—it tended to work out because she had five overbearing, determined and with-it older siblings to help her clean up her messes.

The fact that she'd spent most of her adult life—which wasn't a huge amount of time considering she was only twenty-five—trying to create some distance, some independence from her family was something she'd been proud of. She certainly didn't *want* someone always sweeping in and cleaning up her messes. She wanted to prove to the people who'd raised her from the time she was eight and her parents had disappeared that she could take care of herself.

Too bad she'd finally gotten herself into a jam no one could save her from. She took a deep breath of the cold, invigorating air. Winter held the Hudson Ranch in its grips and for the first time in her life Anna wasn't wishing for spring. Or summer.

Especially not summer.

She closed her eyes, willing the nausea away. Her

doctor—not her *normal* doctor, because even doctor-patient confidentiality wasn't safe in Sunrise, Wyoming, but the doctor she'd found the county over—had told her "morning" sickness could hit at any time and last possibly her whole pregnancy.

Three months in was definitely enough for Anna, but her baby didn't seem to be getting the memo.

So far, she'd been able to keep everything on the downlow, but the more unpredictable the nausea and food aversion got, the harder it was to hide.

She couldn't conceal it forever. Realistically, she understood that. In practice? She'd given herself three months. She considered that fair. Lots of women waited to announce their pregnancy until they were into their second trimester.

The problem was her secret was getting harder and harder to keep. She lived with too many people, had too many friends. And the three-month mark had come and gone.

Surely she could wait until she started to show? That seemed fair. Her family would be upset, but...

"You okay?"

Anna jerked. She hadn't heard Cash approach. She turned to face him and forced herself to smile. She couldn't throw up in front of him. That would be too much. Someone would insist she see a doctor, and then...

"You aren't...pregnant, are you?" he asked very, *very* carefully, and out of nowhere to Anna's estimation.

Of all the people she'd expected to call her out on it, her brothers had been at the bottom of her list. Particularly Cash, who didn't even live at the main house and kept his nose out of her business the most out of any Hudson—

though that was still pretty nosy. Still, Cash didn't butt in, for the most part. He had his own daughter to raise.

She supposed it made sense, though. Since he *was* a dad. Izzy was eleven, and her mom hadn't stuck around for long, but once upon a time, Cash had been the attentive husband to his pregnant wife. So of all the people in her life, he'd been the closest to the signs of pregnancy the most recently.

"Hell in a handbasket, Anna," he muttered when she didn't answer.

She swallowed down all that wanted to come up. "I don't see what business it is of yours." Bravado was often the best response to her overbearing siblings. Or had been.

Cash rolled his eyes. "You wouldn't." He adjusted his hat on his head. "Who knows about this? Certainly not Jack or we'd have had a shotgun wedding by now." His frown deepened. "You're not even dating anyone."

She smiled at her brother, because an off-putting offense was always the best defense. "I know you're a monk and all, but there is this thing called a *one-night stand.*"

He swore again, taking off his hat and raking his hand through his hair. "Who is it?" he demanded, all furious and older-brotherly.

Anna didn't shrink in on herself, though she kind of wanted to. Pregnancy was making her weak. She sniffed and lifted her chin instead. "None of your business."

"Why not?"

Anna had always considered Cash the most reasonable of her brothers. Jack and Grant were the upstanding stick-in-the-muds, Palmer was more like her—or had been before he'd decided to go fall in love with her best friend—and Cash was…the reasonable one. The single dad who kept an even keel no matter what went wrong. His typical response to anything was to hunker down.

But the look on his face was decidedly unreasonable and bloodthirsty.

"I don't need you wading in to fix my problems, Cash. I can handle this."

Cash's expression changed. She realized he might be the calm one, but he was also the worst one to find out about this. Because he'd been in an accidental pregnancy situation himself. As the father of the baby.

"You told the guy, right?" he said. Very carefully. All cool and detached while his eyes were hot with his own issues.

Anna decided silence was her best weapon. But that only made Cash swear even more.

"Anna, you gotta tell the guy."

She shrugged jerkily, because anyone telling her what she had to do grated. Especially when they were right. "Why?"

"Because it's his kid, too."

There was no argument to be had here. First, Cash wasn't the audience. Second, she knew she had to tell the father. Every night she told herself tomorrow would be the day.

And every morning, she chickened out. Not her usual MO, but Hawk Steele was a *problem*.

"He isn't local."

"So take a trip," Cash replied. Firmly.

And she had to blame it on pregnancy hormones. Because she was not a soft woman. She'd learned to be hard. She'd lost her parents at eight, and though her sister had tried to fill in as a kind of maternal influence, Mary was only two years older than she was. So Anna had learned how to be tough, how to be a Hudson.

She'd done the rodeo. She was a licensed private investigator. She'd fought people, shot people, been shot at.

She didn't cry.

But there were tears in her eyes now, even if she managed to blink them away. "Cash, I can do this on my own. Well, not my *own*. But I have you guys. We'll be all right."

Cash inhaled, then pulled her into a hug. Because he had a little girl, and he was a good dad, and he knew how to comfort better than any of them. "We will be, Anna. No matter what." He pulled back, fixed her with a stare that made her wonder if her parents would just despair of her if they were still around. "But he has to know. You've got to give him a chance to be all right, too."

"I know. I do. I just…" Well, bottom line was she just didn't want to. She had always handled guys easily. She had four older brothers, plenty of family trauma. Guys had never scared her, never gotten the upper hand on her. She enjoyed the ones she wanted, then discarded. And had lived that way quite happily and carefully…

Until she'd met Hawk Steele's dark blue gaze across the room at a bar. She'd been handling a private investigation case, away from Sunrise and away from her family, and he had…

She'd *never* felt that way. And as tough girl as she liked to pretend, she'd never had a one-night stand before. They hadn't even exchanged last names at the time. There'd just been something elemental. *Necessary*.

And she'd been foolish enough to forget all her rules. To forget *everything*. Until she'd woken up in his bed, wrapped up in him, knowing she had to get the hell out before…something.

She hadn't been surprised when he'd shown up in her life a little while later. Because of course she'd looked him up after that night. It wasn't hard to track down a guy named Hawk in Bent County, Wyoming. Especially when, it turned out, he *worked* for Bent County as a fire investigator.

So when her friend Louisa's family home burned down before Christmas, Anna had figured she'd end up running into Hawk Steele. She'd practiced her casual, flirty smile. Her unwavering *I don't care about you* bravado. And it had worked. When they'd run into each other, she'd been calm and cool.

He had been shocked. For a second. But a second of shock on Hawk Steele *was* something.

"I can come with you," Cash offered, bringing her back to the present.

It was a sweet offer. She wouldn't take it, but for the time being, she'd let him believe she might. "Thanks. I'll… He kind of travels around, so I'll see if I can pin him down for a meeting." She pulled back from Cash's hug, flashed him a smile. "Promise."

"Look, if you need me to, I can cover your chores. Izzy can help out a little more with the dogs. Then I can—"

"No. I'm good."

"You don't want to overdo it."

"I know. I listen to all my doctor's many instructions." She looked up at the gray winter sky. The Hudson Ranch had been in their family for generations. Though all of them worked on their pet project—Hudson Sibling Solutions, solving cold cases for people like them who didn't have answers—the ranch was their foundation. The six of them worked together to keep it going.

Because her parents had. And her grandparents. And so on.

"Mom handled all this stuff when she was pregnant with me, right?" Anna said, waving her hand around the stables and the cows and the mountains that made up her life, her roots. "That's the memory. Supermom doing ranch work and taking care of all of us and… I bet she never…" Anna couldn't finish the sentence. She rarely thought of her mother, only remembered odd flashes of a strong, warm woman who'd always made her feel safe.

Until she and Dad had just been…gone one day.

"She was supermom," Cash agreed. "But, first of all, we were kids and she was an adult, so we don't really know what she had going on or didn't. Second, and take it from someone who spent a lot of years trying to be Dad, you don't have to be the parents ours were. You just have to be the one that's best for your kid."

Kid. She still really didn't quite think of whatever was growing inside her as a *kid*. Or herself as a parent. Maybe that was just another thing she was putting off.

"I've got chores to do. Then I'm heading out of town for a few days," Anna said firmly. Because she'd already decided that, and she wasn't changing any plans just because Cash had found her out. "And before you lecture me, it's just research. Nothing dangerous."

Cash's frown was epic, but she was used to big-brother admonitions over her side job.

"I don't think you should keep doing your private investigation work."

"And I don't recall asking your opinion. I told my boss

I'm taking a break from the bounties and stuff like that for a while, and that I didn't want to travel as much. This is a simple gathering of some adultery evidence over in Wilde. Take some pictures. Hand them over to the PI office. The end."

"I don't like it."

"Didn't ask you to."

Cash blew out a breath. "Fine, but for the love of God, tell Jack about this before you go. I do not want to be the secret keeper."

"But you're so good at it!"

He groaned as she walked away, laughing. Because… Well, Hawk was a multilevel problem, sure, but Cash was right. She'd be okay. She always was.

ANNA DIDN'T LIKE to admit that pregnancy had an effect on her body. But after a day of driving around trying to catch some salesman cozying up with his pretty lawyer, and coming up empty, Anna was exhausted. And since Wilde was too small to have even a nearby B and B, she'd had to drive over to Fairmont to find a place to stay.

Since she was going under the radar, she stayed at a run-down little motel a few miles outside of Fairmont. Not her first choice, but it was one night and she could sleep one night anywhere, especially as exhausted as she was.

She thought dimly about calling up Hawk. She didn't have his cell or personal number, but she had his work number. After watching him handle Louisa's fire case, she knew he was enough of a workaholic to probably answer even after hours.

But she was too tired. Maybe she'd wake up early and call him.

She crawled into the dingy bed, not even bothering to shower. She'd handle it all in the morning. She was always a good sleeper, so it was no shock when she fell into an almost immediate sleep.

She woke up to a coughing fit. When she blinked her eyes open, they started to sting. It was dark, but something was wrong. Her throat burned. It was too warm. And… it smelled like fire.

She leaped out of the bed in the same motion she swept the phone on the nightstand into her hand. She didn't know where the fire was coming from, but there was one. She ran for the door, grabbed the handle and pushed, thinking it would give, because of course it would. But it didn't, so she just rammed right into it. She twisted the dead bolt, then tried again, but nothing happened. The door was stuck.

The knob wasn't hot, though, so the fire was coming from…somewhere inside. Smoke was filling the room, so she crouched, trying to find some better air to breathe.

She didn't panic. Couldn't. She dialed 911 on her phone while still turning the lock and knob. There was no window in this room. There was one in the bathroom, but she was afraid that was the source of the smoke.

Someone picked up, but before she could even get out a word, something hit her head. Hard. So hard she only had a moment to try to brace her fall before the world went dark.

When she woke up, she was in a hospital bed.

She blinked at all the blinding white. Everything was fuzzy. Groggy. Had the fire been a dream? Was *this* a dream?

She didn't know how long she existed in this odd in-between state before it felt like she was really with it. Before she understood and started to remember.

Panic slammed into her. The fire. Her baby. She put her hands on her stomach, but she didn't know if it was any different. She didn't know…

She looked wildly around the room, expecting to see the familiar face of one of her siblings or at least a doctor.

Instead, standing at the foot of her bed was the one person she didn't want to see.

Chapter Two

Hawk Steele considered himself a man who rolled with the punches. After all, life had been nothing but a series of them. He liked to think he'd come out pretty well, all things considered.

Then Anna Hudson had entered his life. She was more of a gut punch. Or maybe a knee right to the balls. Had been since he'd seen her across the room at Rightful Claim all those months ago. He'd stopped at the saloon in Bent, Wyoming, after a particularly difficult case, looking for a few drinks and maybe a pretty woman to take his mind off it.

He'd found both, but of course, Anna Hudson was no simple pretty woman. The fierce, immediate attraction had blown him off his axis. He'd been relieved when he'd woken up the next morning to find her gone.

Uncharacteristically floored when he'd run into her in Sunrise a while later when he'd been investigating a case that had involved her friend and her brother.

But that flooring had *nothing* on this one. Because he'd heard her brother out there. Very clearly mentioning that Anna was *pregnant*.

Pregnant.

He wanted to believe that this was a coincidence. Sure,

he'd had an ill-advised one-night stand a few months ago with the smart-mouthed beauty, not knowing his life would ever connect with hers again. But that didn't mean *he* had to be the father. Maybe she'd had quite a few careless nights with quite a few men over the course of the past few months.

But the way she looked at him now was answer enough.

And Hawk did not know how to deal with that very hard and unexpected punch. Except rely on the one thing that got him through it all. Stoicism.

"So, Blondie, sounds like we have a lot to catch up on."

She hadn't moved, but now she very slowly—and clearly attempting to make it look casual—took her hands off her stomach. "What are you doing here? Where's my family? I need to…" She swallowed. "Talk to a doctor."

"Doctor will be in soon enough. Family is in the waiting room, wreaking their usual havoc. The nurses said you'd be coming out of the sedative and I wanted to be able to ask you some questions right away."

"But…" Her eyebrows drew together. "There was a fire."

"Yes."

"You want to ask me questions about the fire." She looked around the room one more time, shifting in the bed. He tried not to notice how pale she was. Tried not to think about what might have caused that bandage on her head.

She met his gaze, though it flickered with none of her usual confidence. "I'm having a hard time believing Jack let you in here alone."

"He was in here, but then he got a call about the case and stepped out so as not to interrupt your sleep."

"Ah."

Hawk knew he didn't have much time left. He wasn't sure he believed in divine intervention, but if he did, he supposed this was it. "Were you going to tell me?" he asked. When he should probably ask a million other things, but he needed to know this one first. He just did.

She swallowed, and he saw a million answers flash in her hazel eyes. But he didn't know how to believe any of them as the truth.

"I was working on it," she said, her voice hoarse.

Hawk said nothing to that. He'd been standing here watching her sleep for something close to an hour, trying to convince himself this wouldn't be personal. It would be an arson investigation—because it had clearly been arson. A fire started specifically in the room Anna had rented for the night.

But she'd been so still, so lifeless, in this bed. The bandage on her head where someone had hit her over the head and left her to die in a fire. It had taken him almost the entire hour just to deal with his rage over that.

He still couldn't fully grasp the whole *baby* thing.

And he didn't have to. Because the door opened and Jack Hudson strode in, looking thunderous. He was wearing his Sunrise Sheriff's Department uniform, slightly more casual than a county deputy, but Jack Hudson made it look like military whites.

He was a man who seemed to demand respect wherever he went. Under normal circumstances, Hawk would have respected it.

But sheriff or no, he was Anna's older brother. And Hawk didn't do the whole family thing. The Hudsons were a big messy mix of personalities and demands, and he'd had quite enough of them just dealing with the O'Brien fire and subsequent issues last month.

They were like a *circus*. Hawk had built a life of order.

Anna Hudson his one and only deviation. One that was supposed to have been temporary.

Anna looked at Jack. Her expression was heartbreakingly young-looking. None of her usual bravado when she spoke to her brother.

"Is…? Am I okay?" Her hands crept over her belly again. Her stomach. Where *his* child grew.

Child.

That had definitely not been in the plans, ever. Someone didn't get abandoned by their own father as a fetus to repeat the cycle. At least he didn't.

If that was his baby, then Anna Hudson was no temporary problem. She was his. For life.

"THE DOCTOR WILL be in in a few," Jack said. He had his cop face on and Anna knew it was for Hawk's benefit. She also knew him well enough to know that little tic in his jaw was a clear sign he was *very* much not okay. "He'll go over the specifics with you, but luckily most of the reason you were hospitalized is the head injury."

"Head…" She reached up, but Jack crossed too quickly and took her hand in his. He gave her a reassuring squeeze. "We'll get to the bottom of it. Investigator Steele is going to lead the arson case," Jack said, nodding at Hawk. "Bent County will work with him on the assault angle, and Sunrise will offer whatever manpower we can."

Anna wasn't sure she cared about all that. Not until the doctor came in. Not until she knew… "Jack?"

"The baby's fine," he said. Stiffly. Quietly. As if he was

embarrassed, because Anna was *sure* he had to feel that way. Embarrassed and disappointed and ashamed, and not wanting a stranger to the family to know.

Little did Jack know that stranger had something to do with it.

"Can I just answer his questions and then…?" Anna slid a glance at Hawk.

Hawk raised an eyebrow. No doubt knowing what she'd meant to say. *And then he can go and leave me alone.* Because she was hurt and confused and fuzzy, and she didn't know how to keep up her walls when it came to him.

She needed space until she did.

Jack turned to Hawk. "Why don't you give us a few minutes? Until after the doctor checks her out."

"If I recall, we agreed I could be in here so I could ask questions right away. So we get everything as fresh as possible." Because of course a man like Hawk wouldn't give her space or time.

"Well, what have you been doing?" Jack demanded.

Hawk chose not to answer that question and fixed those midnight blue eyes on her. "Take me through what you remember about last night."

"I had a job in Wilde. I didn't get anything, so I was spending the night at the motel so I could head back out tomorrow. Had to go to Fairmont to find a place." Anna walked him through everything she remembered, but she got to the motel in her memory and then everything kind of went hazy and blank. "I remember waking up to smoke, but that's it." She furrowed her brow, trying to find something in all that haze. "That's it," she repeated, feeling like a failure.

Hawk nodded and was clearly not thrilled with those

answers, but he surprised her by not pressing her with further questions. "All right. Well, you all have my information if you think of anything else or if you remember any other details." He turned to Jack. "I'll keep you updated on the investigation as necessary." Then his gaze returned to her in the hospital bed. There was the tiniest flash where his gaze drifted to her stomach, so tiny she almost missed it.

"I'll be in touch," he said darkly. Definitely more threat than promise.

But Anna felt like she could breathe once he was gone. She knew it wasn't over. So many parts of this weren't over, but so many things now had happened at once and she had to untangle them. Piece by piece.

Starting with Jack. Who was standing there, a few paces away, looking ominous. He was ten years older than her. He'd been a father figure to her longer than her father had been. He was their…leader, as much as Anna hated to be led.

And she knew, she *knew* he would not be happy about this. How could he not be disappointed in her keeping this secret? His disapproval she could weather, but his disappointment was too much to bear.

"So," he said, finally breaking the silence. "You thought it would be a good idea to tell Cash and no one else."

Jack did always know how to twist the knife when he wanted to. "If it makes you feel better, I didn't *tell* Cash. He figured it out. Besides, the father didn't exactly know before today either."

"What do you mean, didn't…?" Jack looked back at the door. Then a wave of pain crossed his face. "Him?"

Anna didn't bother to answer.

"Anna. Damn it all to hell." He shook his head. But he was Jack, so… "What's the plan, then?"

"The plan?"

"Are you going to get married?"

Anna burst out laughing, which maybe wasn't the right response, but it was the only one she had. "Hi, I'd like to introduce you to the twenty-first century."

"I think it's a fair question. And it was a question, not an assumption or demand."

"But you'd like to demand it."

"I'd like to know that…" He inhaled sharply. "That you're okay, and that you have a plan."

"I don't need a plan to be okay."

His mouth firmed. Disapprovingly. Which was hardly a first. Usually she kind of lived to earn his disapproval. But there was something about this moment, or the cascade of them, or the whole hormone thing and fire thing, that coalesced and it just felt awful.

Unbearable. So that the tears started and wouldn't stop.

She hated that she was crying, but each of her siblings played a role in her life. Oh, she loved to torture Jack in any way she could, because he was wound so tight and all. But he was also her safe place. Her parents had disappeared when she'd been eight, and Jack had stepped into that hole. He'd never once faltered. Not for her.

So if she was going to lose it—those damn pregnancy hormones, she was sure—it was going to be with Jack. Not anyone else.

"Would they hate me?"

He looked as taken aback by that question as he was by her tears. "Would *who* hate you?"

"Our parents. They'd be disappointed, right? They'd think I did it all wrong and—"

He was across the room and crouched next to her bed, eye to eye, so fast she didn't even have time to finish her sentence.

"Listen to me," he said fiercely. "Our parents weren't perfect. I...I tend to remember them that way because that's the nature of things, but they were normal people with flaws and mistakes. But I know... The one thing I'm damn sure of is that whatever concern or upset they might have felt, and that's a big *might*, you'd never have known, Anna. Because they would have supported you. They would have been there for you, no matter what. Just like we will be."

Which of course only made her cry harder. Because it was so ridiculous she hadn't told anyone. She knew that her family was always there for her. No matter what.

"Annie." And she only ever let Jack call her Annie. Just like Mom had done. Only when it mattered. "Someone locked you in that room. Someone bashed you in the head. Someone set that fire in the room *you* rented. This was no accident. No mistake. Someone wants you dead. So there's got to be a plan. To make sure you're safe."

Chapter Three

Hawk studied the remnants of the burned-down motel room. He'd already been through it once, but it was always good to go through an arson scene a few times, just to make sure you didn't miss anything.

The elements had done their number, but it didn't matter. The more he could get a picture of it in his head, the better chance he had to get to the bottom of it.

But that was part of the problem, too. He had to picture it. That was his job. But usually he could picture a faceless, nameless victim. A mannequin stand-in to keep him from feeling anything.

But all he could see was Anna with her blond hair, sprawled out on the ground, while a fire crept toward her. Only a well-timed 911 call and a trackable phone had kept her from being burned alive.

Purposefully.

Because that fire had been started in room 104. Anna's door lock had been tampered with. Someone had used a lamp to knock her out.

And left her to die.

Hawk saw a lot of bad things in his line of work. He was excellent at keeping up that wall between fury over the terrible things people were capable of and doing what needed to be done.

It didn't surprise him in the least to be struggling with that when it came to Anna Hudson. Her entire existence seemed hell-bent on making sure everything involving her screwed with who he usually was, what he usually did. *All* his plans.

Because he was going to be a father. And he was very well aware that was as much his own fault as hers, but who else would he have made such a mistake with?

Except he wasn't going to think about this situation as a *mistake*. Maybe it was unplanned, but not a *mistake*. No doubt he had a father out there somewhere who'd viewed him that way. Who'd gotten the hell out before he'd had to deal with the consequences. At best, Hawk had a sperm donor.

And these thirty-two years later, it still bothered him. He'd had the best mom in the world, by his estimation, but even she hadn't been able to fill that hole. He'd known he was missing something, always. Especially when she'd gotten sick and he'd had to pick up the slack.

His child wouldn't have one second of that. Not if he could help it.

"Steele."

Hawk looked up at the man who walked toward him, very nearly catching him off guard. Hawk let his hand slide off the butt of his gun in a casual move as the Bent County sheriff's detective approached. He'd worked with Thomas Hart a few times and was glad to see a familiar face. "Hart."

"Unfortunately, there's no video footage of the parking lot or the rooms, just the main office. Clerk claims she didn't see anything."

"I was afraid of that." He'd already talked to the clerk himself and gotten a similar story. He had the sneaking suspicion that the clerk had been drunk or high on something and truthfully didn't remember or notice anything that happened. Maybe ever.

"I'm heading over to Ms. Hudson's employer's office. Fool's Gold Private Investigations. I figured you'd be headed there too, so we might as well team up."

"Yeah, that was my next stop." He should have left a good twenty minutes ago, instead of brooding over an arson scene.

"I've already talked to Ms. Hudson's boss there. She's expecting us."

"I'll follow you."

Hart nodded and Hawk pulled himself away from the remains. He had the lab running some tests on a few pieces of evidence he'd found, but it would take time. So he needed to pound the pavement while everything was still fresh. There was no rest until he got to the bottom of this.

Because this wasn't his average investigation—and not just because he tended to deal with fraud or onetime fire starters, and this was clearly a targeted assault. It was because it was Anna and his baby.

And the threat was still out there until they figured out who had done it and why.

Hawk followed the Bent County cruiser down the highway to the small town of Wilde. Wilde was even tinier than Bent *and* Sunrise. It didn't have much other than a few churches and a convenience store, and—in an old brick building—the fairly newly minted Fool's Gold Private Investigations.

Hawk parallel parked behind Hart, and they got out of their cars at the same time and met in front of the building.

"You're from around here, right?" he asked Deputy Hart, who nodded. "You know anything about them?" Hawk gestured at the building.

"In a complicated sort of way," Hart replied, pulling the door open. "The lady that runs it is my cousin's husband's brother's girlfriend." Hart shrugged. "You know, that sort of thing."

Hawk decidedly did *not* know that sort of thing. The minute his mother had died when he'd been fourteen, he'd been without family. A thing very few people around these parts seemed capable of grasping.

The building was nice. It looked almost like it had once been a bank with the tiled floors and old-fashioned counters with windows. A young woman got up and skirted the counters. She was dressed casually, wore no jewelry and had a very tough demeanor. She walked with the hint of a limp.

"Quinn Peterson." She gave Hawk a firm shake with her hand, then fisted it on her hip. "Obviously I've heard the rumbles, and I know Anna was hurt. I'm ticked as hell about it. Whatever I can do to help the investigation, I will. Particularly if it ends up relating to one of the cases she's taken for us."

"Thanks," Hawk replied. "We're looking into anyone who might have had motivation to hurt Ms. Hudson." *The mother of my future child.* He had to push that thought away and focus. "So one of the leads is—"

"Any case she worked on that might have gone sour or

made her a target. I get it. And I'd love to hand over all my files for you, or have a clear-cut answer, but unfortunately, I don't. We're a private investigation company for women, by women." Quinn shrugged, unbothered. There was something slightly off about her, but not…wrong, per se. Just different. "Sometimes a woman just feels more comfortable getting help from a woman. I don't like to turn people away, so I've got a couple of people who do part-time work for me since I can't be everywhere at once. Anna Hudson is one of them. She's a hell of an investigator, and what's more, I like her as a person."

"Then we'd like to look at those files," Hawk replied. So far, Quinn Peterson played everything just right, but that didn't mean Hawk would let his guard down. He understood privacy, understood why she'd want to keep those files to herself, but it couldn't happen.

"I want to help you get to the bottom of this as much as anybody, but I have to protect my clients, so I can't just hand over my files. What I can do is give you a list of anyone who might have been upset by work Anna did for us and offer my help to investigate them in any way that might help you guys."

Hawk knew he'd get that answer, but he didn't have to like it. It would take him days to potentially get a search warrant, and even that would only fly if he could get a lead to prove the need for one. "Would Anna have her own files?"

"We keep professional files here, but anyone can keep their own personal files, and if she wanted to hand those over to you guys, that'd be her choice." Quinn crossed her arms over her chest as if to punctuate the fact that he wasn't getting her files.

Hawk didn't see much point trying to change Quinn's mind. She didn't strike him as the kind of woman bowled over by charm *or* authority. She was running a *private* investigation company, after all.

He handed Quinn his card. "Email me that list when you've got it."

"Me too," Hart added.

Hawk didn't scowl, though he wanted to. He'd prefer to handle this case all on his own, but there was an assault and he knew he needed to work with the police as he so often did.

Quinn took the card and nodded. "I'll get right on it." She looked up at Hawk. "I do want to help, even if it's not in the way you'd like."

Hawk didn't sigh despite the urge. He kept it professional. "Thanks."

It felt a bit like a waste of a trip. He could have done all that over the phone, but it was good to get a sense of people. He didn't have any bad feelings about Quinn, but he'd see what kind of list she came up with.

He walked back outside with Hart.

"Quinn's legit," Hart said, pausing at his car and slipping on some sunglasses. "I know you've got to look into her, and she'd expect you to. So it's no big deal. But I wouldn't spend too much time on a dead end."

Hawk agreed, but he didn't acknowledge that. "You're leaning more toward someone she investigated that maybe got the bad end of it?"

"That'd be the most straightforward, wouldn't it? Anytime one of us cops gets threats, we start by looking at people we arrested. This situation is about the same."

About the same. Except Anna was pregnant with his child.

Would he ever be able to set that aside and get his job done?

"I'm going to head back to the station. My partner's on maternity leave, so I've got to juggle some things around. But the minute Quinn's email comes in, I'll start looking."

"Okay." Hawk squinted at the sky, thinking. He knew Hart was waiting for him to explain what he was going to do. It grated, but eventually he relented.

"I'm going to get her personal files." If he had to steal them out of the Hudsons' house, he would.

ANNA WAS BACK HOME, THANKFULLY. The doctor had said the baby was doing A-OK, and while Anna needed to take it easy because she'd suffered a concussion—not her first, thanks to a few years in the rodeo—and because of the smoke inhalation, she was also in decent shape considering everything she'd gone through.

Of course, her family was now treating her like she was made of fragile glass. Mary had arranged her on the couch with enough pillows and blankets to suffocate a grizzly. She'd been given water and snacks and Mary had even insisted they all eat dinner in the living room on tray tables so she didn't have to sit at the dinner table or eat alone.

No one brought up the fire, her injuries or the whole baby situation point-blank. She appreciated it at first, but then it started to feel like this odd weight on her chest. An elephant in the room that reminded her way too much of those early days after her parents' disappearance when there had been hushed whispers and awkward silences and no one wanting to say what was going on.

So after dessert, but before everyone scattered as they often did this time of night, Anna decided to go ahead and wade right in.

"Well." She surveyed her family. Now not just her four brothers and one sister and one niece, but Grant's girl-friend, Dahlia, and Anna's best friend from childhood, Louisa, who was somehow hooked up with Palmer. There were dogs everywhere, because Cash raised and trained them and one of them had just had puppies two months ago.

"I'm due in June," she said, trying not to look too closely at anyone's reaction. She'd already had her little meltdown in front of Jack, so this wasn't going to be a repeat. Just facts. Just…the truth. "I don't quite have all the plans made yet, of course, but… You know, there's time to deal with that. So…"

She didn't want to mention Hawk. No doubt everyone knew now, and had opinions about it, but if she didn't mention it…

"I can't believe you're having a baby with Hawk Steele," Palmer muttered.

Which earned him an elbow in the side from Louisa. Louisa glared disapprovingly at Palmer. "Hawk turned out to be very helpful with our case."

"Yeah, after he investigated *me* for the fire at your folks' place," Palmer returned. "And he hasn't apologized," Palmer noted.

"He does not seem like the kind of guy who apologizes readily," Louisa said, chewing on her bottom lip. But she smiled encouragingly at Anna. "It doesn't matter. Because it's Anna and Hawk's business. *Not* ours."

It was nice to have her friend support her, proving that having your best friend date your brother wasn't *all* bad if she took your side in family arguments.

"It's because he's so handsome."

Everyone turned to look at Izzy, who had two puppies on her lap, and had dropped that little truth bomb very casually.

"What did you just say?" Cash demanded.

She looked up at her father. Clearly confused by his tone. "What? He's handsome. Like Levi Jones."

"Who the hell is Levi Jones?"

Izzy rolled her eyes dramatically. "Oh my *God*, Dad. Do you pay attention to music at *all*?"

"Your dad's more the Willie Nelson type," Palmer said with a laugh, enjoying his niece's impatience with her father.

"Besides, Hawk is way better-looking than Levi Jones," Mary said primly. Which earned her a glare from all four brothers. Mary only shrugged in return.

"What is wrong with you?" Cash asked.

"Nothing is wrong with her," Dahlia returned in her quiet way. "I quite agree."

"Like way hotter," Louisa piped up, sending Anna a wink so Anna would know she was purposefully riling up the menfolk. Usually Anna's job. "Hawk Steele is distressingly hot."

It was Palmer's turn to look offended, there with his arm around Louisa's shoulders. "Excuse me?"

Louisa grinned up at him. "I love you, honey, but that

doesn't mean I've gone blind. Don't worry. You're hot, too."

Anna appreciated how uncomfortable her brothers were with this line of conversation, how Louisa was attempting to entertain her, but as she was trying very hard *not* to think about how good Hawk looked, she needed to nip this conversation in the bud. "Hawk Steele is—"

"Right here."

Anna whirled her head around to look over her shoulder. Hawk stood next to Grant, who'd apparently left the room and let him inside at some point during the conversation.

Anna was not easily embarrassed. She usually found situations like this pretty funny. But…not right now. This was just embarrassing.

Mary stood. "Are you hungry, Mr. Steele? We've got plenty of leftovers. Still warm. It'd be no trouble to make you a plate."

"I'm fine, thanks. I just needed to discuss some things with Anna."

"Of course. We'll give you your privacy." Mary sent everyone in the living room a pointed look that clearly told them to leave.

"We will?" Palmer and Jack said in unison, which would have been more annoying if Palmer didn't look quite so horrified he'd said the same thing as Jack. But Mary could play drill sergeant when she wanted to. She marshaled everyone out of the living room, eventually leaving Hawk and her alone.

Aside from the puppy Izzy had dropped on Anna's lap on her way out.

Hawk stared at the puppy, an unreadable expression on his face.

"I talked to Quinn Peterson today. She refused to give me files of the cases you've worked on."

"Of course she did," Anna returned, trying to not be surprised he'd come to talk about the case. About *business*. Of course that was all he was here for. What else mattered in the moment? "Those people don't need to get dragged into this."

"'This' being an attempted murder investigation? *Your* attempted murder."

She rolled her eyes at him. "Yeah, that. I'll give you a list of people I might have ticked off by exposing their bad behavior, but Quinn's not going to give you her files. I won't ask her to, and even if I would, she'd say no. It's a matter of privacy and integrity."

His mouth firmed, clearly not pleased with that answer. "I'm already getting that list from Quinn, but comparing and contrasting wouldn't be bad. Nevertheless, list or no, you'll give me your personal files."

Anna stared at him for a beat, waiting. When he didn't continue, she scratched the puppy's belly and raised an eyebrow at him. "Or what?"

"What do you mean, or what? That's it. You'll give me your files."

"Because you said so?" she asked, her voice deceptively mild as she cradled the puppy to her chest. Honestly, puppies were smarter than men sometimes.

"Yeah, because I said so," he replied, then frowned deeply at the puppy in her arms as she got to her feet.

"Well, Hawk." She crossed to him, handed him the puppy. She knew he didn't want it, but he took it because he didn't know what else to do. Or because she had been hurt and that gave her just enough of an edge for him to do things she wanted him to do.

She smiled up at him, though she assumed it looked as unpleasant as she felt.

"Go to hell." Then she turned and walked out of the room.

Chapter Four

Hawk could admit when he'd handled a situation badly. Maybe he didn't know Anna well, but he knew enough not to order her around. He didn't know too many women who reacted well to bossiness, but Anna Hudson was *really, clearly* never going to respond well to *anyone* trying to tell her what to do.

Now he was standing in an empty living room holding a puppy, wondering how everything had gotten so derailed.

But she'd been all wrapped up in blankets and pillows, family and friends all waiting on her and cheering her up—clearly that whole conversation on his attractiveness had been a kind of bit to rile up her brothers. And it had worked. They'd been riled and Anna had been laughing and her friend had been grinning and…

He'd known he didn't belong here. Interrupting. Being the father of anyone's child.

But he was. Whether he *belonged* or not. It wasn't about his comfort or his belonging. It was about facts—and the fact was, Anna was having *his* child. He and Anna needed to discuss what that was going to mean.

And she needed to hand over her files so he could keep her safe.

He needed to get back on his normal footing first. Get

in the right headspace. He couldn't keep making these mistakes when it came to her. *Why* did she bring them out in him?

He could go home and regroup or he could just follow her to wherever she'd gone. Sure, it wasn't his house, but he was trying to figure out who was trying to *kill* her. He could take some liberties.

He turned, determined to do just that, but stopped short.

Anna's sister stood there, with that bland, pleasant hostess smile on her face. He supposed Mary and Anna resembled each other, though Mary had darker features, and was a bit taller and willowier, but there was something in the shape of the eyes and nose that clearly signaled they were related.

As far as Hawk could tell, that was about the only similarities the women shared. Mary was always the consummate hostess. Every time he'd come to the Hudson Ranch—and it was almost always without warning regarding a case—Mary was always soft-spoken and carefully, femininely dressed. She always offered a drink or a snack and nothing but kind words.

But there was something about the way Mary stood in his way that had him feeling oddly...uneasy. And like the sisters might be more alike than they appeared.

"Oh, are you going to adopt him?" she asked hopefully.

"What now?"

"We are *drowning* in puppies. Cash can only keep and train so many, so we're looking for a few good people to take the extras." Mary beamed at him. "This one seems to have taken a shine to you."

Hawk looked down at the black-and-brown animal who

was currently trying to chew at his coat's zipper. Take the puppy? Was she insane? "No, I..."

"Why don't you take him for a trial run? I'm sure you're a busy man, so if *really* you can't fit him into your life, you can always bring him back. But he's got all his shots and he's halfway to potty-trained. You never know until you try. Right?"

"Halfway?"

"He's a smart cookie, aren't you?" she cooed, scratching the puppy's ears. Mary looked up at him, pleasant smile firmly in place. "And I'm sure you are, too. If Jack trusts you to run this arson investigation, you must be."

"Well, I—"

"Then you're just the person to take him," Mary said with a firm nod. "As far as I know, he doesn't have a name, because no one can agree on what to call him. You can call him whatever you like."

"No, I..." But he was being maneuvered. Away from the living room and the hallway Anna had disappeared down. Mary was herding him toward the front door.

She ushered him right to it. The puppy wriggling in his arms. He turned to firmly tell her he was not taking this dog. To put the dog down on the ground. Mary could get rid of Hawk if she really wanted to, but he was not going to wind up with this dog.

"Besides," she continued, opening the door and then stepping so close to him he had no choice but to retreat. Out into the cold. "A puppy is sort of like a *start* toward learning how to take care of a baby. Don't you think?"

He opened his mouth but no sound came out. She closed the door firmly in his face.

Before he could say or do something, the door reopened.

He almost felt relief—this was some kind of prank. Giving him a hard time because of the whole Anna-being-pregnant thing. He could take a prank. He could handle a little ribbing.

But Mary was holding a big plastic bin and she placed it firmly in front of him on the porch. "Can't forget the supplies!" she offered cheerfully.

The door slammed this time and the dead bolt clicked firmly and loudly into place. No prank. No joke.

The puppy in his arms whimpered. Then proceeded to pee on his coat.

"Fantastic," Hawk muttered, with no earthly clue what to do. Except drive home with a pee-covered coat…and a puppy.

ANNA WAS TUCKED into her bed, and Mary was lying next to her like they'd done a million times as kids, relaying the story of the look on Hawk's face when she compared the puppy to a baby. Mary was laughing and it made Anna feel warm and fuzzy.

Her whole life had been a strange dichotomy of loss and so much luck and love it made her head spin. She'd lost her parents at a young age, and there'd been a lot of suffering because of that. But her siblings had always been there for her. No matter what. She had an amazing family, and it was part of why even though the pregnancy had been a surprise, she'd always known she wanted to keep the baby.

"Have you thought about names?" Mary asked, rolling onto her side to study Anna.

Anna stared at the ceiling. Thinking about names meant thinking about reality, and she'd rather think about Mary insisting Hawk keep the puppy. "I've barely even thought about what I'm going to eat for breakfast tomorrow, Mary."

"Well, I'm going with you to your next appointment. Unless…"

"Unless what?" Anna asked, tugging at her sheet in an effort not to look at Mary.

"Well, maybe Hawk will want to go."

Anna glanced over at her sister, who was now examining the comforter. "I don't exactly get strong daddy vibes from the guy." He'd come out all this way and not even *mentioned* the baby. Just her case files.

The jerk.

Mary raised an eyebrow. "Oh, really? I got *very* strong daddy vibes." Then she waggled her eyebrows, shocking a laugh out of Anna, because usually Mary was very prim and proper and above those kinds of jokes Anna and Louisa enjoyed.

But she was trying to make Anna laugh, Anna understood. Because Mary was the mother of the family, no matter her age or place in it. She wanted to make Anna feel better, and she knew all the tricks to do it.

Anna would say Mary should be the one who was pregnant, but Mary would never be so irresponsible as to start something without a plan. To catch the eye of a stranger across the bar and lose herself in a night of…

Well, *that* did not do thinking about.

"I'll let you get some sleep. But you come get me if you need anything."

"It was a bump, Mary," Anna said, touching the bandage on her head. "I'm fine. Doctor said so."

Mary slid off the bed and she tried to smile, but Anna

knew her sister too well. She didn't say anything, but she didn't have to.

Until they figured out who'd hurt her, Mary would worry. Mary said good-night and Anna did her best to force a smile.

She was going to need to take control of this situation. The whole attempted-murder thing. The whole...baby thing.

She slid her hand over her stomach. It was still hard to believe. Even when she heard the little *womp, womp, womp* of the heartbeat at the doctor's office, or watched the little wriggle of lumps on the ultrasound screen.

She'd been living in denial, more or less, and she couldn't anymore. Because her family didn't need to be worrying over her. Because growing a baby was important, but so was surviving whoever wanted to hurt her.

So, in the morning, she got dressed and ate breakfast with everyone, and then, even though she hadn't expressly told anyone she was leaving, and okay, maybe *sneaked* off the ranch making sure no one saw her, she drove over to Hawk's place in Bent.

He had a cute little house on Main Street, that much she knew. Of course, she'd only seen both inside and outside in the dark, and she'd been a little...occupied on the inside.

Today, she noted a leash tied to the porch, though no puppy on the end. The sun was just beginning its trudge up in the sky, fighting off January gray. It was early, so she hoped he hadn't gone into work yet, but who knew what an arson investigator's hours were.

Maybe she should just go back home. He was either sleeping or busy or—

Stop being a coward, Anna.

She forced her feet to move. They had a lot to deal with and now they were going to deal with it. On *her* terms. Not his directives. She had a plan in place. A list of things to discuss and talk about.

Mostly about the case, because as far as she was concerned, they still had five months to deal with…the rest.

She knocked on the door, maybe harder than necessary. Immediately the sharp yips of a puppy sounded from inside. Then a crash. Then the door slammed open.

He was shirtless, disheveled, and looked like he hadn't shaved in a day or two with a dark shadow of whiskers doing nothing to hide the sharp jaw. His blue eyes were hotly furious, and he definitely looked like he hadn't slept much. The puppy was running in circles, creating a mess of shredded toilet paper as he yapped and jumped and ran behind Hawk.

Hawk glared. "I blame *you* for this nightmare."

Her mouth was too dry to speak. How…*how* could a man be such a mess and look so damn hot? He was lean but muscled. *Rangy*, she supposed, was the word. She knew this. She'd seen him naked, but maybe she'd tried to convince herself her memory was flawed. No man could be that hot.

He had a little tattoo, right over his heart. A hawk, of all things.

She wanted to kiss it.

When she managed to pull her gaze up to meet his, his eyes changed, that dark blue deepening. Just like it had done that first night. Across the bar. Before they'd ever said anything to each other. Just *bam*. Instant, destructive *lust*.

Her breathing had gone shallow. Every nerve ending seemed to braid itself underneath her skin. Just like then.

It would be foolish to follow that same path. Wrong, with everything they had to deal with. She was in danger, so there were *far* more important things at hand than scratching an itch she'd already once scratched.

But… "You know, I'm already pregnant," she managed, though her throat was tight. Her heart echoing loudly in her ears. Loud enough to drown out rational thought, clearly. Her body pulsing with all that sudden need she'd only ever felt so sharply, so *out of nowhere* with him.

"I do know that. Now."

"So, whatever we did…or didn't do, here, in this moment, wouldn't have the consequences it once did. They've already…*consequenced*."

He raised an eyebrow, that dark blue gaze raking over her like a touch. *Please go ahead and touch.*

"That an invitation?" he asked, and she hoped she wasn't hallucinating that there was a new edge to his voice that hadn't been there before.

"Maybe."

He jerked her to him, just like he had the first night. It wasn't rough so much as the tipping point. Something about being alone, something about *them* ignited. She dived her fingers into his hair, curling and holding on as he devoured her mouth with his. He kicked the door shut, then lifted her, and she wrapped her legs around him as he moved her deeper into the house.

Into the bedroom, onto his bed. The puppy yipped excitedly from somewhere behind them, but Anna could not have cared less in the moment. He laid her down on the bed, then paused and just looked at her.

"I don't know what the hell this is," he said, but he was pulling off her boots. Her jeans. Everything in quick, efficient movements.

She pulled off her own shirt since his was already off. "That makes two of us."

"Well, at least there's that." He unclasped her bra, ran his big, rough hands down her body, and then he was on top of her, inside her.

And it was just like the last time. All heat, all combustion. A crazy need she didn't understand. Mutual and encompassing. So it was like what they created between them was its own world and only the two of them knew about it, understood it.

Like this connection had been planted in them long ago, before they'd laid eyes on each other. Hell, maybe before the earth had taken its first rotation around the sun. It felt that big, that weighty.

That right.

And it was that thought that settled into her as he took her over the edge and followed.

Chapter Five

Hawk had long ago forged himself into a person who didn't make mistakes. When his mom had been sick, when he'd done everything to keep her going that he could think of, he'd determined he'd only make the *right* choices. For her.

And even after she'd died, he'd kept that promise to himself, because what else had there been to do? Either keep the promise or just…give up. Giving up felt like too much of a betrayal of everything she'd given him, so he'd worked hard and done the right thing. So that in whatever thing happened after death, she was proud of him.

Then Anna Hudson had come along. Damn, she was beautiful. All spread out in his bed, self-satisfied smirk on her face and nothing else. And he couldn't categorize her as a mistake, exactly. She seemed too…inevitable. Something ignited between them, and maybe it didn't make any sense, but it was…there. Real.

And would likely have him making a few mistakes before all was said and done. Still, it seemed a good time to make it clear he had plans. Naked. Happy. Relaxed.

"I think we should get married," he said idly, toying with the ends of her silky hair as he contemplated his ceiling.

"What?" It came out like a screech.

He glanced over at her. "You heard me."

She leveraged up on her elbows and glared at him, though, truth be told, he had a hard time looking at her eyes. "You do not want to get *married*," she said.

"I believe I said I did."

"Hawk, that's…insane. You do not seem like a draconian, knuckle-dragging, backward-thinking chauvinist."

"You don't know me, Anna." Not that he was any of those things, but he just wanted to make sure to point out that she didn't have him pegged. Couldn't. When they'd spent all of a handful of hours together.

"No, I don't. Which is why I won't be *marrying* you. My *God*. You're as bad as Jack."

"So Jack would agree with me?" He could use the older-brother angle if he had to.

"Jack agrees with the primordial ooze, and this has nothing to do with my brother." She slid out of bed and began to hunt for her clothes, putting them on as she found them. He just watched her move around his room…the puppy chasing her and nipping at every item of clothing she picked up.

"So what does it have to do with?" Hawk asked casually. He wasn't going to make the same kind of mistakes he'd made last night. No demanding. No getting caught off guard with families and puppies. Just calm, rational propositions.

"Sanity?" Anna replied. Sadly, she was dressed now, and she picked up the wriggling, yipping beast he'd been saddled with, who had already trashed his house and somehow had ended up sleeping on his pillow last night.

"Have you fed him?"

"I've done every damn thing I can think of with that

creature, but he is a spawn of Satan bent on destruction." They'd even gone on a walk up and down Main Street last night. He'd bought a dog toy at the general store and tried to teach him to play fetch.

He'd bought him *treats*, since Mary's bin of junk had come with food and a leash and a few other necessities but nothing else.

Anna cuddled the puppy close, and he licked her chin as she tsked Hawk. He sat up in the bed. She'd looked so clean and fresh when she'd shown up at his doorstep. Now she was flushed and rumpled.

He really didn't have time for a round two.

But it was tempting.

Still, it was best to press his case when she was still here. Softened by the puppy and good sex. "I grew up without a father because he bailed. I'm not repeating the cycle."

She didn't have anything to say to that for a good few seconds. But she regrouped quickly. "Okay, but that doesn't mean we have to be *married*."

"I happen to think it does. No custody BS. You and me and the kid, Blondie. We'll make it work."

"How?"

"By deciding to."

She stared at him for a very long time, then shook her head. "Hawk, this isn't happening."

He pointed at the spot she'd vacated on his bed. "The sex is good."

"The sex is great. That's not a reason to get married."

He didn't preen at her calling it great, but he didn't hate it either. "I imagine people get married for less." He slid out of bed, didn't miss the way she watched him. And maybe he took his sweet time crossing to his dresser and grabbing a new pair of boxers for her benefit.

"I came here to talk about the case," she said, sounding like she had at the door. A little strangled, a little breathless.

"That is *not* what it seemed like."

"Well, you were all shirtless and disheveled. So sue me for taking a detour. Why do you have a hawk tattoo? Is Hawk even your real name?"

He tried not to tense. "Yeah, it's my real name."

"And you felt the need to get the pictorial form of your own name tattooed over your heart?"

"I did." He pulled on a pair of sweatpants. He'd need to run through the shower before his first meeting of the day, but he had some phone calls to make to the lab first. He glanced at his clock. It'd open in about fifteen minutes. So if he could get her to agree with him and shoo her out of here by then…

"You expect me to marry you, not knowing a thing about you, while you also act completely unwilling to *let* me know anything about you?"

It was a fair point. He didn't like it, but it was fair. So he turned to face her. Shrugged casually. "My mom liked hawks. She was into all this spiritual junk, thought they were her spirit guides or something. That's why she named me Hawk." He didn't pause, because it would give too much space for…emotions. "I got the tattoo when she died."

Anna's eyes softened. That was the thing about her. She acted all tough, brash and like she didn't have a care in the world. After that first night, and the fact she'd been the one to sneak out afterward, he would have been sure she truly didn't.

But he'd watched her with her siblings since. He'd seen her comfort her best friend when Louisa O'Brien's family home had burned down. There was a sweet heart underneath all that barbed wire.

Maybe it was wrong to focus on that, but he'd use it to get what he wanted. What was *necessary*.

"How old were you?" she asked, petting the puppy thoughtfully.

"Fourteen." He'd gleaned enough information about the Hudsons to know the parents weren't around. "You?"

"I'm not sure. My parents disappeared when I was eight. Don't know if they died or what. Hence the whole Hudson Sibling Solutions thing we do."

"Hell."

"Yeah, it was. But I had my siblings." She studied him for a long time. "You have anybody?"

He could lie. Evade. But he thought the truth was pretty clear. "Nah."

She nodded. "I was never planning on, like, keeping you out of it." She didn't quite meet his gaze. "I was just being a coward about the whole thing. So I'm sorry about that."

He shrugged. He'd never seen much use for apologies. They didn't change a damn thing. "No harm done, I guess."

She stepped forward so they were closer, but her eyes were soft and imploring. "But that doesn't mean we should get married. Marriage is about…loving somebody," she said earnestly.

He didn't know about that. He couldn't say he'd ever

been around a happily married couple for very long. But he did know one thing. "Aren't we going to love the kid?"

ANNA KNEW THERE had to be a good response to that question. One that reaffirmed how absolutely ridiculous it was to think they could get married just because they'd created a child, when they were virtual strangers.

Because *of course* they'd love their kid, but a marriage "for the kid" looked different than a marriage because you fell in love with someone.

Didn't it?

"Look—" But she didn't have a chance to say anything else, because something on his face changed and he held up his hand. She might have argued with him—no one held up their hand to her to stop her from talking—but it was something about the way he narrowed his eyes, reached over into the same drawer he'd pulled boxers out of and produced a gun.

"Get in the bathroom," he said, pointing to a door off to the side. "The only window in there is small."

"Hawk—"

"Take the dog with you," he said sharply. Then he disappeared out of his room.

She was not good at doing what she was told, but she was a private investigator, sister to a cop. She knew something about how people reacted to danger and threats, and maybe she hadn't sensed one.

But Hawk had. She trusted that he had, but she didn't like being relegated to bathroom hider. He was a fire investigator. Lived here alone. If he had a gun in his dresser, he likely had other ones.

She looked around the room. The dresser was too far

from the bed for that to be the only weapon he had in here. If he was worried about threats, he had to have one within reach from where he slept. She went over to the nightstand, pulled open the drawer. There was an assortment of things—a bottle of aspirin, some sort of medal she'd be interested to inspect later, some cords, and an old-looking, pocket-size book with no title on the cover. Another thing she wanted to inspect, but now was not the time, because behind all that was a small gun.

She shifted the puppy into the crook of one arm, pulled out the gun and checked it. Loaded. "He's going to have to learn some gun safety if he wants to have a kid around here," she muttered to keep her nerves from vibrating out of control.

She moved to the room door, peeking out to survey the living area. The front door was wide open and she didn't see anyone, so she moved into the room. She'd almost made it to the door when Hawk strode in.

He didn't even chastise her for not listening or ask where she'd gotten the gun. "Call 911 from my landline," he said, pointing to an old-fashioned phone on the wall. "Your truck's on fire." He grabbed a fire extinguisher from a cabinet in the kitchen.

"Hawk, you can't… That's a small, indoor extinguisher. What's it going to do?" But she was dialing 911 on the phone.

"Not much, but I know fire. I've got to stop it before it spreads. Stay put. Keep him put, too."

She tightened her grip on the puppy, then relayed all the information she knew to the 911 operator. Once the operator had everything she needed, Anna left the gun on the counter and hurried back to the front door to see how Hawk was faring.

He'd clearly gone through the entire extinguisher, but her truck was still in flames. Some neighbors had come out and Hawk was ordering them all around. Buckets and hoses appeared.

She took one step—just *one* out onto the front porch—and Hawk immediately lifted his gaze to hers. "Do not come out here. Stay out of the smoke."

It was only because of the baby, and because she'd just inhaled too much smoke a few nights ago, that she listened. She closed the door and watched from the window as a cop car appeared, and then a fire truck.

It took time, but they finally got the fire out. Hawk stayed outside talking to neighbors, firefighters, a cop who looked to be about the same age as him and she thought maybe she recognized from her work. When Hawk finally got rid of everyone and came inside, he was sweating and dirty. His eyes were red, and he had a bandage around one hand.

"Oh, you hurt yourself!" She reached forward, as if she was going to do what? Someone had already bandaged it and she wasn't going to kiss and make it better. She dropped her hand and looked up at him.

He had an odd expression, but it quickly smoothed out into that professional I'm-Mister-Arson-Investigator-And-Smartest-Man-In-All-The-Land blankness. "Someone torched your truck. On purpose."

"Yeah, I picked up on that."

He wiped his sweaty forehead on his forearm. But it just smeared soot everywhere. "I called your brother."

She didn't groan, though she desperately wanted to. "You shouldn't have done that."

He shook his head. "Don't be stubborn, Anna. Someone is after you."

"They had to know I wasn't *in* my truck, so they were hardly trying to burn me alive."

"This time. *This* time. Because it's the *second* time, Anna. The first time they did clearly want you dead. So it doesn't matter this time whether they wanted you dead, hurt or scared—it isn't *good*."

She tried to ignore the jitter of fear that went through her at the harsh way he said it. "Sure, but we're…figuring out who."

"Not we, Anna. You'll leave this to the professionals."

The man was truly a piece of work. "I *am* a professional, Hawk."

He scraped his fingers through his hair. He needed a shower. Breakfast. And not to be such a jerk. She figured it wouldn't do to tell him what he needed, so she kept it to herself.

"You know what I mean."

"No, I don't."

"I'm not arguing with you about this."

"Well, if you think you're going to bundle me up and send me home with my brother, you inhaled more smoke than I thought."

"No, I don't think you should go home."

"You think I should stay here?" she asked incredulously. It was one thing if it was about sex, but this was about…protecting her? No, protecting the baby.

"No, I think you should hide."

Anna recoiled. *Hide*. "Hudsons don't hide."

"Well, maybe pregnant ones should."

They were squaring off in his living room. He was all sooty and sweaty, and she was perfectly fine, except for the rising tide of nausea she was desperately trying to ignore.

And worse, so much worse, the little wiggle of softness at the idea that he wanted to protect her. Even as she convinced herself he was only wanting to protect the current vessel of his child, she felt that warmth.

You are a fool, Anna Hudson.

A fool who usually preferred a fight. To wear down her opponent until she got her way. Because she always won. Always got her way.

She had the very frightening thought that Hawk might not wear down as easily as her siblings. She swallowed. "Go take a shower. I'll make us something to eat."

"Listen—"

"It's either that or I lose whatever's left in my stomach from yesterday all over this hideous carpet right here."

His mouth firmed. "We'll eat first. I'm not letting you out of my sight until your brother gets here. You might not like it. Hell, I don't like it for you, but you cannot be alone until we figure out who did this. And before you lecture me about your skills and accomplishments and strengths and blah, blah, blah, I don't care. I would recommend anyone in the same situation—you know, the one where someone tried to *kill you*—not to be alone."

Then he turned on a heel and marched into the kitchen. "Now, what would settle your stomach?"

Chapter Six

Anna decided on scrambled eggs and a piece of plain toast. Hawk insisted she sit while he made it, then made himself some coffee since he hadn't had any this morning. He watched Anna as she ate, making sure she did indeed put something in her stomach.

As for himself, he still wasn't ready to eat, so he sneaked little bites of toast to the puppy under the table.

"Have you named him yet?" Anna asked. She'd gotten a little green there for a few minutes but was looking steadier now.

"Yeah. I think I'll call him Pita."

"Like the bread?" she asked in confusion.

"No, like *pain in the—*"

"Hawk," she admonished. "You cannot name him that."

"If your family is forcing me to take a dog I don't want, I can in fact name him that."

She looked at him for a very long time, so long and so serious, he had the very unfamiliar need to fidget in his chair.

"I think we both know no one could *force you* to do anything."

Something twisted in his chest, a kind of premonition type feeling his mother would have called spirit guidance or divine intuition or something equally out there. Hawk figured it was just enough experience to know such statements were usually challenges to the universe to prove a person wrong.

He'd like the universe to stay off his back, thank you very much.

Anna cleared her throat and looked away. "That's a terrible habit to teach him, you know," Anna said, pointing to where he'd just slipped another piece of bread to the dog. "And breakfast is the most important meal of the day. *You* should be eating it."

"I've been taking care of myself since I was fourteen, Blondie. I can handle it."

Before she could say anything to that, the doorbell rang, followed by an insistent knocking. "I'm assuming that's your brother."

She sighed. "You really shouldn't have called him." She pushed back from the table the same time he did. Which meant they were facing each other, with his little kitchen table between them. He didn't turn to exit the kitchen like he should have. Something about that hazel gaze was like getting skewered, hooked, *something* painful and tangled.

She batted her eyelashes. "Thinking about me naked?"

He couldn't stop himself from grinning, even as the pounding on the door increased. "You're something else, Blondie." But he sobered, because…she *was* carrying his child. And even if she wasn't… Maybe they didn't know each other, but there was *something* between them. Whatever that was that sparked to life every time they made eye contact. Maybe it was just lust, but lust didn't happen with everyone.

"I'm going to do whatever I think needs to be done to keep you safe. I don't need you to like it."

Her flirtatious smile faded, not to the scowl he expected. Disapproving, sure, but softer. She opened her mouth to say something, but Hawk was pretty sure her brother was going to break down his front door if he didn't go answer it. He moved past her and into the living room, the puppy at his heels.

She followed but stopped in the middle of the room, which he realized she must have tidied when he'd been outside fighting the fire because the evidence of the puppy's war with toilet paper was gone.

"I...thought you'd call Jack," Anna said softly as she caught sight of her brother in the sidelight.

"Figured you'd prefer to deal with this one." He opened the door and Palmer stepped in without waiting for an invitation.

"What the *hell* is going on?" Palmer demanded. He looked at Hawk, then Anna. He pointed his finger at her. "You sneaked out this morning."

"I hardly sneaked."

"I have cameras on the property, Anna. You *sneaked. And* turned off your phone."

Hawk gave her a sharp look, but she only shrugged. Leave it to the woman in danger to be a hardheaded problem.

And carrying your child.

"I don't like this," Palmer said, crossing his arms over his chest. Echoing Hawk's thoughts exactly.

"Join the club," Hawk muttered.

Pita took up an unholy racket, trying to bark intimidatingly at Palmer. Who only reached down and scooped up the puppy and patted his rump. The fearsome guard dog whimpered happily and snuggled in.

"She's being targeted, and it's going to take some time to investigate. I called you over here, not just because her truck is totaled, but because I'm recommending you all tuck her away somewhere safe until we have even one clue as to what's happening and why." Hawk would have preferred to be the one tucking her away, but he was going to be too busy investigating to keep her under lock and key.

God knew she needed twenty-four-hour supervision or she'd end up doing something reckless.

Palmer studied Hawk, then Anna. "Great in theory, but have you met her?"

Anna smirked.

But before Hawk could deal with that, Palmer turned a heavy stare on him. "You sure this doesn't have anything to do with you?"

It took Hawk a few seconds to fully understand what Palmer was getting at, it was so insane. "Me? I wasn't anywhere near that motel. Who would target me through her?"

Palmer shrugged in that lazy way Hawk figured was as much an act as anything. "I don't know, but fire seems right up your alley."

ANNA WAS STILL marveling over the fact that Hawk had called Palmer—who was indeed the brother she'd rather deal with if she was being forced to deal with one. Palmer was overprotective and obnoxious in his own way, but he could at least take a joke. Make light of things now and again. He didn't get all bent out of shape when she poked at him.

He'd been the one to convince Jack to let her go to the rodeo. He understood her better than the other three.

But she didn't like him trying to turn the blame toward Hawk. "I think I make far more sense as a target, as the only way anyone would have connected me with Hawk was to know we hooked up one night three months ago."

Palmer made a face, no doubt at the words *hooked up*, which had *maybe* been Anna's intention.

"I'd also like to note to both you pig heads, pregnancy doesn't make me incapable of taking care of myself."

"Then explain the other night," Hawk and Palmer said in unison.

It was Anna's turn to pull a face. "For the love of God, don't start sounding like each other." She shuddered. Then she straightened her shoulders and faced them both down.

"I can be reasonable. Especially since I imagine it's a little rough to try to shoot while puking your guts out, which still happens on occasion. But I don't want anyone talking around me like you have to wrap me up in Bubble Wrap or send me away like some ancient damsel in distress. I'm also an investigator, and I'm damn well going to investigate who's after me."

Both men opened their mouths, no doubt to argue with her, but she knew how to deal with men.

Or at least her brother.

"But, because of the pregnancy, I will make one concession. I won't do anything alone. Someone can be by my side at all times. But not you," she said, pointing at Palmer.

"You want Jack or Grant?" Palmer returned incredulously, Cash obviously off the table since he had a daughter to take care of. And Mary didn't handle any of their cold case investigations and preferred to stay on the administrative side of things and avoid guns and blood when she could.

"No." She jutted her chin toward Hawk. "This guy here says he wants to marry me."

Palmer's jaw nearly dropped to the floor, which entertained the hell out of Anna.

"I happen to think it's a terrible plan," Anna continued, undeterred by Hawk's intimidating scowl. "So we'll be all cozy together while we investigate this little problem, and at the end of things, we'll either prove a partnership like marriage is a good plan—" she flashed him a grin "—or we'll all agree it's a *terrible* one and get on with our lives."

"You're not tagging along on an official investigation," Hawk said.

"That's cute you think you could stop me."

His eyes narrowed and, much like when they'd been back in his bedroom, darkened.

Why was he *so* hot? It was really distracting when she was trying to one-up him and irritate him at the same time.

"You should probably go take a shower while Palmer's here to babysit me," Anna offered, trying to arrange her features to look innocent and angelic.

She watched him fight with the desire to say something or be Mr. Taciturn. The latter won and he turned without saying anything and disappeared into the hallway to his bedroom.

"Anna, you've sure gotten yourself into a mess," Palmer muttered, scratching the puppy in his arms behind the ears. Pita's tongue lolled out in ecstasy.

"Yeah." And it wasn't just the whole someone wanting her dead thing either.

"You're not seriously going to consider marrying the guy, even if this investigation *does* go well."

She knew she should say "absolutely not." She knew she should feel that. But all she could think about was the way he'd stared at the wall when she'd asked him if he had anyone and he'd said *nah*. She looked at her brother. "He doesn't have anyone, Palmer. He's all alone."

"Maybe that's because he's a jerk. You can't just… marry him because you feel sorry for him."

"No. I'm pretty sure at the end of this he'll realize the last thing he wants is to be saddled with *me* as a wife."

Palmer was quiet for a minute, then reached over and gave her hair a little tug like he'd done back when they were rodeoing together and she'd lost spectacularly. "You're not such a bad prize."

She wasn't so sure about that, but there was no point arguing it. She was going to make sure Hawk didn't want to marry her anymore and would be convinced it was his idea all in one fell swoop. "It'll be good." She nodded firmly, as if to convince herself. "We'll figure out who's after me and he'll realize there are better ways to deal with this whole baby thing."

Chapter Seven

Hawk took his time in the shower, even though it was strange to know there were people out there in his house. There were *never* people in his house. He didn't bring women here—Anna being the one and only exception. If he did things with friends, he never invited anyone back here.

He'd never given much thought to why that was. It just seemed natural. To keep to himself. To be…isolated. He *preferred* being alone. He preferred his privacy, not having near-strangers—even if one was the mother of his future child—tromping about his house.

But he needed to weigh his options in some kind of silence and privacy, and Anna needed someone to keep an eye on her. She was acting like she might be reasonable, but Hawk didn't trust her just yet.

It was unimaginable to have Anna tagging along on his actual, professional, by-the-law investigation. He couldn't let her, for a wide variety of reasons that weren't even all personal.

But she was, in fairness, a licensed private investigator. It was about five hundred different conflicts of interest since she was the victim in the case, *and* the mother of his unborn child, but she had experience.

Frustrated with not being certain of the next right move

to make, Hawk wrenched off the shower faucet. He had meetings, calls to make and now *two* arsons to investigate. Not to mention deal with Bent County Sheriff's Department on the assault angle. He didn't have time to let Anna tag along and keep his eye on her.

He also didn't have time to argue with her hard head. But he could leave that up to her siblings. No doubt they were experts.

He toweled off, ignoring the odd ache in his chest. He didn't know what that was like. Siblings. Family. Big messy feelings and complications.

Thank God he didn't know what it was like. Losing his mother had been excruciating enough. Why would he want more possibilities for that? He stepped out of the bathroom and into his bedroom.

The puppy was waiting for him in a compliant sitting position, which didn't suit the ornery little minion at all.

He stared at the dog. He did not want it, but the puppy wagged his little tail and looked up at him with dark brown eyes, and what the hell was Hawk supposed to do? Tell Mary to take him back?

"Your name *is* Pita," he muttered as he crossed to his closet and began to get dressed for his meetings and consider his approach to Anna and her brother.

He'd throw her a bone, certainly. He'd allow her to help with some elements of the investigation. She had the best insight into who might be after her, so it made sense, and it would make her feel like she had a say. Feeling like you had a say was always important.

But he needed to make sure she agreed to a situation where she was never alone. He considered having her move in here, but then he'd have to take her with him wherever he went and that wouldn't fly for when he was interviewing people he didn't want her around.

The ideal situation would be her tucked away somewhere secret, with one of her siblings standing guard. In his experience, the people in these far-flung western towns *always* knew someone with a tiny, off-the-grid cabin to hide away at.

But again, the guard was an issue. No doubt her brothers would protect her, but Anna had a lifetime of learning how to outsmart them. Hawk wouldn't be able to relax in that situation.

Still mulling over his options, he returned to the living room. He had an appointment to make, so this would have to wait.

But before he could say anything to Palmer or Anna, she fixed him with a bright, wide smile he didn't trust at all.

"We've come to a bit of a compromise."

"That so," Hawk returned, eyeing the puppy, who had trotted over to the couch and was sniffing the leg.

"You'll come stay at the ranch," she said. "Cash can help you train Pita. I can work with you on the case, and someone will always be around to keep an eye on the knocked-up target."

Before he could say anything, Palmer started talking. Clearly, they were ganging up on him.

"We've got good security all around the ranch, and I can beef it up. It might have been Anna's truck that was targeted, but it *was* in your driveway. Which means someone might be connecting you to this. You both under one roof, with lots of eyes and security. It makes sense."

Hawk hated to admit that it did, that it wasn't the worst

plan. And he could tell they really didn't expect him to go for it. Which made him perversely eager to agree.

He wanted nothing to do with the Hudson circus, but this also accomplished a few goals. He'd have Anna constantly underfoot to work on her about the whole getting-married thing. He'd always be able to leave her behind and know someone was watching out for her, even if he brought her into a few investigative things. Plus, he liked the idea of security. Not so much for his own safety, but because any lead—including someone trying to target him—would bring them closer to answers.

He'd prefer her farther away, somewhere secret and isolated, but this was indeed a compromise.

"Okay," he agreed. Easily and without one argument. He had to bite back a smile at the look of shock on their faces. "I've got some meetings, so you can take Anna on back to the ranch. After I get my work done, I'll pack up and be on over to the ranch this evening."

"I should go with you," Anna said, frowning.

Hawk moved past her and picked up Pita's leash. He affixed it to the puppy's collar. "No." He pushed the door open and took the puppy out to do his business, Anna following behind him.

"I *am* going to be part of this investigation, Hawk." She didn't look at the burned remnants of her truck, but then again, neither did he. It felt better to ignore it, and a lot of things, in this moment.

"You should go home, Anna. Make me that list of people who might want to hurt you. *That* will help me with my investigation and make you a part of it." Pita did a little squat, right on the concrete. Hawk scowled. Couldn't even pee in the grass like a normal dog.

"An investigation you've told me nothing about."

He raised an eyebrow at her. "You didn't exactly give me a chance to this morning," he returned. Pointedly. Pointedly enough Palmer groaned behind Anna. "Besides, you didn't give me your files."

"And I won't," she returned mulishly, crossing her arms over her chest. "It's an invasion of privacy. But I'll get you a list."

"Fantastic. So you have your job today, and I'll go do mine. In perfect agreement." He smiled at her. "I'll see you tonight at the ranch."

She narrowed her eyes, scowling, and he was a smart man, so he knew better than to believe her silent exit was going to be *good* for him. Palmer's low whistle and pat on the back as he passed to follow her to his truck only sank that dread further.

"You've got a lot to learn, pal," Palmer muttered.

Hawk watched them get in Palmer's truck and leave. A lot to learn. He supposed about Anna and figuring out how to be a dad, he did.

But when it came to investigating arson, he was the best. And that was the most important thing to focus on today. He glanced at the puppy, who was currently sitting at his feet and chewing on the laces of his shoes.

"Well, Pita. Looks like you're my partner today."

BACK HOME AT the ranch, Anna put together her list. People she'd investigated or bounty hunted who might want to target her and were out of jail or alive enough to do so. She created little dossiers on all of them, ranking them from smartest to dumbest, violent to not even knowing which end of a gun the bullet came out of, and in the end ranked them from most likely to least likely.

Then she emailed it to Hawk *and* the Bent County detective. "Take that, hotshot investigator."

Once she'd done all that work, she wasn't sure if she was more hungry or exhausted. Growing a baby was *hard*.

She yawned. She'd just crawl under her covers for like five minutes and then go get some food. Then she'd go find Hawk. Trail him through his investigation. She could probably figure out everyone he was talking to today.

But when she blinked her eyes back open, the room was dark.

And, just like when she'd woken up at the hospital, a man was standing at the end of her bed.

"Your sister said you were in charge of determining where I'd sleep."

"Oh." Anna tried to get her brain to engage. Tried to think past the way he looked in a suit, his tie loosened as though it had been a hard day. "Well, there's room here." She patted the space on the bed next to her and smiled at him.

Hawk's eyes narrowed and darkened, even in the dim light. Quite the lethal combination. Did the people he interrogated find themselves unreasonably turned on?

"I might not know anything about family dynamics, but I'm not sleeping in the same room with you under your brother's roof," he said.

Poking at her temper, whether he meant to or not, Anna wasn't sure. "It's my roof too, buddy."

"Be that as it may, not happening."

She considered. She didn't want to put him in the guest room. It was far away from hers, and she wouldn't get her whole point across. It needed to feel like they were on top of each other. He needed to be around her constantly enough to be annoyed by her. "I thought you wanted to get married."

"Well, unless we're heading over to the courthouse tomorrow, that's a moot point."

"Not for me. I could hardly marry someone I haven't lived with. This is actually perfect. It doesn't have to be messy with joint leases and copies of keys. It's like a trial run." She smirked up at him. "If I can stand to share a room with you in this big house, maybe, just maybe, I could entertain the thought of marrying you." *Or make you run screaming in the opposite direction.*

He didn't immediately argue, though he did look at her with a heap of suspicion. "I'm not having sex with you with your entire family all around."

She grinned at him, because *sure.* "Mind in the gutter, Hawk. I just need to know if you're a cover hog. What time is it, anyway?" She glanced at her nightstand clock. "Time for dinner. Good—I'm starved." She got out of bed and grabbed his arm as she passed him.

"I already ate," he said, standing firm when she tried to tug him along with her.

She laughed. "Like that matters. Staying under the Hudson roof means you are required to attend Hudson dinner. It's the law." She tugged harder this time, and he reluctantly moved with her out of the room and down the hallway.

"I never agreed to follow Hudson law."

"It doesn't require your agreement. That's the beauty of it." She let him go but hooked her arm with his as they descended the stairs. "So. Get any leads today?"

There was a slight hesitation, no more than a fraction

of a second, but she was investigator and woman enough to know he'd considered lying to her. But in the end, he told her the truth, and she had to be *not* warmed by that. Because he'd thought about lying to her, and that should matter.

But it didn't right now.

"No. But I cross-referenced your list with Quinn Peterson's. Almost identical. First few weren't immediate possibilities, so we'll go down the line. Shouldn't take more than a day or two to get initial impressions, and by that time I should have some of my lab reports back from the crime scene."

"Bent County would have other lab reports, right? Yours would be fire. Theirs would be attack."

"I work for Bent County, so we'll work together."

Anna nodded. "Quinn told me Thomas Hart is the detective on the case, and she knows him. Said he's good. Jack hasn't worked *with* him, but I guess knows him in that cop way, and was complimentary. Well, as complimentary as Jack ever is."

Hawk nodded in silent confirmation, which Anna figured was practically like a presidential commendation.

"In fact, Hart brought up an interesting point today." Hawk stopped moving, and Anna could have kept pulling, but there was something about his expression that had her stopping.

"Okay."

"We're looking into your work, but we haven't really asked about your personal life."

She wanted to laugh. Make a joke. It was on the tip of her tongue. And if it had been anyone else, she likely would have teased him about wanting to know about her past lovers.

But someone had tried to kill her, and he looked so serious. And he wanted to *marry* her and be a father to their baby because he hadn't had one.

So, she swallowed down her smart replies. "I haven't…" She felt unreasonably exposed by the admission, even though it hadn't been that long. Even though she *had* been busy. She cleared her throat, trying to push away her discomfort. Because the truth was more important than her ego. "I haven't been with anyone, or seen anyone, since that night at the bar."

His eyes deepened, and that answering flutter started low in her stomach. "It was…Christmas," she managed, though her voice came out strangled. "I was busy."

His mouth quirked up, and the flutters turned into something *far* more dangerous. "And before that?"

She shook her head. "I'd have to look through my calendar to know exact dates, but I'd been focused on proving myself at Fool's Gold, so dating hasn't been high on my list."

"Anything that ended badly? No matter how long ago?"

"I mean, I slashed my high school boyfriend's tires when I found another girl's bra in the back of his precious Mustang, but he's now married to said girl, so…" She shrugged. "Come on. Let's go eat."

Anna led him into the big dining room, where they always tried to have dinner together. And everyone was indeed here today—including Dahlia and Louisa. And Cash's menagerie of dogs.

Pita saw or scented Hawk and scrambled over with an excited yip, though they couldn't have been parted for long. Anna had the strangest sensation that at some point, she'd have a kid...who might just get excited at the sight of their father.

Kid.

Father.

"Anna, are you okay?" Mary asked, looking up from where she'd been placing a big bowl of green bean casserole on the table. "You look pale."

"Fine. Just hungry."

"Well, sit. Eat." She smiled encouragingly at Hawk. "If you have any dietary concerns, just let me know. I'll add it to the spreadsheet."

"I...don't. I'll eat anything."

"Fantastic." Mary bustled off to get the finishing touches on dinner together, and Anna gestured Hawk into a seat, trying to shake off the weird feelings plaguing her. There was a lot of time before this baby was a *real* baby, so a lot of time before she had to figure out what to do with the whole father part.

Her only goal now was to convince Hawk he couldn't possibly want to marry her, so he'd stick to that decision.

Oh, and find out who wanted her dead.

"So, Hawk." Jack stared down the table at him, and Jack looked so much like their long-gone father in that moment, Anna's heart turned over with a longing so sharp it nearly made her want to cry.

Until Jack said, "Why don't you update us on the investigation?"

Chapter Eight

Hawk felt like he'd been through the weirdest-ass gaunt-
let he could imagine. He didn't know why he thought he
could handle the Hudsons. It was like trying to handle a
million yapping prairie dogs with the plague.

He had a headache now, and a weird kind of guilt over
quizzing Anna on her past relationships—even though
he shouldn't feel guilty, because that was the job. Worse
than the guilt was some sort of primal, *absurd* satisfac-
tion that there hadn't been anyone after him.

Like that mattered.

Or the way she'd looked, curled up in her bed, fast
asleep. Sweet and vulnerable, while he'd had to breathe
through the knowledge someone had tried to kill her. And
he was no closer to finding out who.

Now Jack wanted to itemize the investigation for the
whole Hudson clan to hear. Uh, no.

"I'm not sure that's appropriate dinner conversation."

"We don't worry too much about appropriate these days,"
Jack countered easily. "Do you have a list of suspects?"

"Whether I do or don't, I won't be sharing that list."

"Why not?"

"Because involvement by any of you could harm not
just the investigation, but the results. You're in law en-

forcement, Jack. You know as well as I do protocol is just as important as answers. When we find the person behind this, there won't be any loopholes. The case will have to be ironclad so they can spend the rest of their lives in jail, where they belong. I can't risk civilian involvement."

"I'm not a civilian," Jack retorted.

"No, but you're not an unbiased party either."

Jack's mouth firmed, but he didn't keep up the argument.

What Hawk didn't know about the Hudsons, he'd made sure to brush up on today. Even though it wasn't part of the case, per se, he'd thought it smart to understand all the players he would be sharing a roof with.

Jack Hudson was indeed the oldest and had raised his siblings after their parents' disappearance. He'd been in the police academy when it had all happened, and stuck with that, working at Bent County for a time, all the while lobbying the town of Sunrise to start their own department. Once they had, he'd run for sheriff. For eight years, he'd been in the top position at Sunrise, and ran a tight ship.

Which meant he should know Hawk was being honest. He couldn't risk the investigation with a lot of Hudson interference.

Mary, who handled not just playing hostess, but apparently all the administrative and accounting tasks for both the ranch and HSS, expertly steered the topic of conversation away from Hawk and investigations and toward other things, like puppies.

Hawk appreciated the help, but he knew that wouldn't be the end of it. He glanced at Anna. She was whip-smart, so fooling her wasn't going to be easy, but he had to make her feel like she was part of the investigation without that actually being the case.

The list she'd emailed him today had been far more thorough than Quinn Peterson's, even if their conclusions were the same. Sadly, of the top two possibilities they'd both chosen, one had been in a holding cell in Denver the night of the motel fire. The other had been in the hospital.

Ironclad alibis.

There were still other names to check into, and he hadn't gotten into asking her family about threats they might see, because Thomas had said that was on his agenda for tomorrow.

Hawk's focus had to be the fires.

Cash and Palmer cleared the table while Mary and Dahlia brought out dessert and conversation zinged around like a Ping-Pong game with five hundred balls. When Hawk glanced to one side, he caught the little girl, Izzy, staring at him. Chin in her hands with a dreamy smile. "Can you play the drums?" she asked him out of nowhere.

"Uh. No."

She sighed as if this was a great disappointment to her. Hawk didn't know what the hell to do with that, so he kept his eyes on his dessert until he was reasonably sure everyone was finished. He risked a glance up at Palmer, who was whispering something into Louisa's ear that made her blush.

Families were weird. "When you get a chance, Palmer, I want to see the security setup."

Anna elbowed him, harder than necessary. "*I* can show it to you."

"I thought that was Palmer's deal."

"It is, for the most part, but I help, so I know. What

exactly is it that you think I do as a private investigator? Google people and pore over their LinkedIn profiles?"

Hawk shrugged easily, because he knew it would ir- ritate her and he wasn't immune to the way she glared at him. "Maybe."

"It's a lot more than that. Especially the cases Fool's Gold takes on. The women who come to us are already close enough to being victims. They don't need more hard- ship. My investigations have to be just as airtight as yours, to protect those people desperate for help."

She was so…passionate about it. It wasn't that it sur- prised him, exactly. She was a woman full of…well, pas- sion. Just that he still didn't know what to do with the way she was comfortable with that passion, that emotion, all those feelings. She just laid it all on the line and never once seemed uncomfortable with it.

He turned to Mary, who was clearly in charge of these dinners, no matter what Jack might think down there at the head of the table.

"I feel like I should help with something," he said. "I've been on my own for a while. I can handle just about any chore you throw at me."

Mary smiled kindly at him. "You will, but you get a day to ease in first. I'll add you to the spreadsheet and give you an overview of your duties tomorrow."

"You seem to have a lot of spreadsheets."

"Oh, Hawk." She got up from her seat and took her empty plate and his. "You have *no* idea." Then she headed for the kitchen, and Izzy and Jack were clearing the rest of the table. Because they clearly all had jobs. He supposed it was the only way a family of this size could function *and* run two businesses together.

"Come on," Anna said at his side. "Let's take a look at the security room."

He nodded and followed her out of the dining room. She led him down the hallway and into a smaller room that had probably once been a utility closet or mudroom at one time. Now it was clearly a security hub for HSS.

Anna went through the whole thing. Computers, cameras, monitors. It was surprisingly high-tech and impressive. The whole ranch wasn't under surveillance, because of the sheer size, but the house and the yard had the capability of being completely watched.

"Is this the result of paranoia or experience?" Hawk asked, watching one of the monitors' grainy view of the porch at night.

"Both, I think," Anna returned, unfazed by the word *paranoia*. "We've had a few people not too happy with the cold cases we've uncovered. That's why Cash tends to keep himself separate. Doesn't want anyone targeting Izzy or him, with her mom out of the picture. It also allows us to offer anyone who hires us protection. When Dahlia hired us, she had someone following her, so we put her up here and the cameras helped us catch some of the people involved."

He studied her profile as she fooled with some keyboard. The idea of her being targeted never failed to feel like a lance of pain right in his gut. But the idea she was always out there, investigating things that might come back to haunt her. He really didn't know how to deal with that.

"Any chance this all connects to the family business?"

Anna looked at him and seemed to consider this possibility with the seriousness it deserved. "It's not impossible. We work together, but we take turns being lead. I haven't led any cases since I took the job at Fool's Gold, so, much like the personal angle—it's possible, but seems less likely."

Hawk nodded. That was the same conclusion he'd reached, but it was good to hear it confirmed. Still, he'd ask her brothers, too. And her friends about anyone in her personal life. Or Hart would, since he didn't have a personal connection to the victim.

Hell, this was a mess. She was an entanglement he was now linked to no matter what and that should be scarier than it was. She was hardheaded, stubborn, volatile, unpredictable, obnoxious and abrasive.

Beautiful. Funny… A constant surprise.

She glanced at him as if she sensed him studying her. She turned her body to face him. She looked just as she had that night at the bar. A challenge in her eyes and something…he just didn't know how to characterize. Like she was enchanted, and he just had to reach out to touch.

"You're thinking about me naked, aren't you?"

If only it were that easy. But he hadn't *not* been doing that either, so what the hell? "Yeah, I am."

"Good."

He'd promised himself this whole living under the Hudson roof meant he was going to be hands-off. He'd promised himself no more funny business until she agreed to marry him. Until they'd made some concrete plans about what having this baby meant.

She led him upstairs and made him break every last promise.

ANNA WAS SURE to be up before Hawk the next morning. Part of her yearned to crawl back into bed and have a repeat performance of last night, but she had plans.

She would have preferred to handle this on her own, but she understood the dangers, her limitations here. Even if no one would give her credit for that. Hard to blame them. Historically, she had *not* been good at knowing her limitations.

Still, just because she couldn't go off and do things on her own didn't mean she couldn't *do* things. She eyed Hawk. He was a deep enough sleeper, it seemed, but he was also an investigator, so it would be hard to pull one over on him.

She scooped up the still-dozing puppy, knowing he'd start barking and running around once she opened the door. She snuggled him close so he was quiet, then moved for the door as if she was going to leave the room. Carefully and casually, she hooked her finger through the loop of Hawk's bag and brought it with her. Quietly, she closed the door behind her, then knelt on the ground. She set Pita down on the rug. "Go on downstairs. Someone will let you outside and give you some food."

His tail wagged happily, but he did not follow instructions. Anna sighed. She left the bag by the door but got up and walked toward the stairs. She kept quietly urging Pita to go down the stairs, but he'd only go down a couple, then zoom back up.

Then one ear perked up and with a yip he zoomed down the stairs. Likely he heard or smelled something going on in the kitchen. Thank goodness.

Anna returned to just outside her door and Hawk's bag. She paused, listening for any sounds coming from her room, but there were none, so she unzipped the bag and pawed through Hawk's things.

The first thing she decided to look at was a notebook

she'd seen him scribble in when he'd been working on Louisa's family's fire. She opened it and frowned. None of what she saw made sense. It was letters and numbers and symbols in some chaotic order.

She flipped to the next page. The same weird mix of letters and symbols. It was written in sentences, even paragraphs, but there was no way of determining what he'd been writing because the order of letters, numbers and symbols didn't make sense.

"What the hell is this?" she muttered, flipping through all the pages and finding nothing but gobbledygook.

"It's my own personal shorthand to keep nosy, conniving people from reading my notes."

She yelped in surprise, nearly tossing the notebook in the air. She glared over her shoulder at where Hawk stood, casually leaning against the door frame. She wasn't sure how he'd managed to open the door so silently, but he had.

"Hardly *conniving*."

"How do I know you didn't use sex to lull me into an exhausted stupor just so you could sneak through my bag?" he returned.

"Trust me, Hawk, the sex is its own reward."

He chuckled at that and something warm and mushy moved through her, because he didn't laugh very often, and when he did, it did things to her. And not even like *want to rip his clothes off* things. Warm, soft things.

He held out his hand to help her to her feet. She let him. Even let him pluck the notebook out of her hand. It wasn't like she could read anything in there.

Once she was standing, he didn't let her hand go. Something in his expression had changed and he studied her with a faint frown. "You cry in your sleep, Blondie."

She froze. "What?" She'd expected him to chastise her for going through his stuff. Not…that.

"Last night. You were crying. I thought you were awake, but finally figured out you were fast asleep."

Her heart jabbed hard against her rib cage, and she had to work very hard to keep her breathing even. "I don't…" It wasn't that she didn't believe him. She knew she did. She just hadn't woken up with a wet face and her own sobs echoing in the room since she was a kid. And whatever she'd been doing last night hadn't woken her up, so she was caught totally unaware. She cleared her throat. "Must be a pregnancy thing." She didn't know if he bought that or not, but she gestured past him into her room. "You're like half-naked here. We might want to go back inside."

He didn't immediately react. Still stood there, blocking the door, one hand on hers and one hand holding the notebook. After a long moment where she felt inexplicably like crying into his shoulder, he dropped her hand and grabbed his bag.

She stepped inside her room behind him, though that didn't feel any safer, and had to forcibly refrain from wrapping her arms around herself. Or worse. Him.

Before she could think of anything to say, something wild and unpredictable that would take his mind off… everything, his phone vibrated on the nightstand.

Still just in his boxers, he crossed to it and held it to his ear. "Steele."

She watched as his face changed. It got that blank cop look, which she'd seen on Jack's face enough to recognize as bad news. But he made some affirmative noises, asked a few questions that led her to believe there'd been a fire somewhere he'd have to go investigate on top of her own.

When he clicked End, he slowly set the phone back down. And expressly did not meet her gaze. Which had her nerves start to jitter.

"There was a fire," Anna supplied for him.

"Yes. Another…possible connection to yours." He sighed and met her gaze. "At Fool's Gold Investigations."

"Quinn—"

"She's fine. No one was in the building when the fire broke out. But I need to get down there and look around. Maybe it's unrelated." He made a move to go to his duffel bag, but Anna stood in his path.

"It's not unrelated."

He sighed and rubbed a hand over his face, the first hint he might be affected by this news in any way. "We don't know until I get down there and investigate."

"It's *related*, Hawk."

"That is the likely scenario, but until I have the facts and evidence, I can't tell you that. Or prove it. So get out of my way so I can get to my job."

"You have to let me come with you." He was already shaking his head, but Anna powered on. "I'll stay out of the way, I promise. But I need to talk to Quinn and I need to… Hawk, I need this. They aren't just targeting me now. My truck, sure, but *your* house. Quinn wasn't hurt, but the place I work for her was. I need to…figure out what the hell I could have done to make someone *so* angry they'd go through all this."

"You didn't have to *do* anything for a person to decide to blame their bad decisions on you. Humans are good at shifting the blame." He reached out, and some survival instinct whispered at her to move away. Not to let him touch her like this.

But she stood rooted to the spot while his hand cupped her cheek. "Don't be good at shifting the blame to yourself, Blondie. It doesn't suit you."

The urge to cry was back, or lean into him, and she could not let her walls down. She might never be able to build them back. She had to focus on the issue at hand.

"Let me come with you, Hawk. I'll only hound Palmer into coming with me if you don't. Then you'll have to deal with both of us."

His mouth firmed into a harsh line. "I could have you both arrested."

Anna shrugged. "Hardly the way to get me to marry you. Not to mention, no one at Bent County is going to issue warrants on that, so it'd be a moot point."

"Anna—"

"I won't get in the way. I *promise*."

"I am going to regret this," he muttered, but it was an agreement, no matter how reluctant. He got dressed, and so did she. Weirdly together in her room. Weirdly, it didn't even feel all that weird.

He handed her a leash. "You're on Pita patrol."

"We could leave him here with Cash and the other dogs if you want."

Hawk shook his head. "If he's going to be my dog, he'll need to get used to being around investigations with me."

Why that warmed her, inside and out, she had no idea.

Chapter Nine

Hawk had figured Anna would be a major distraction, but in the end, she wasn't. She kept Pita from getting in the actual crime scene, and she stood with Quinn Peterson and Quinn's boyfriend, talking to them and keeping them from bothering him while he investigated.

The fire at Fool's Gold Private Investigations had been set in the exact same way as the motel fire, so there was no real hope this was an odd coincidence. No, it was arson, and it was about Anna.

Frustration clawed at him, but Hawk pushed it away and focused on his job. Observing, collecting samples, trying to put the pieces together. He had some theories on accelerant he was hoping the lab would be able to verify today. That would give him another avenue of connections to make.

Then the fact that this was another inside job. Like what had happened in Anna's motel room, it was clear there'd been a break-in followed by the fire starting—somewhere farther into the building than any exits or entrances.

Quinn had given him an outline of her security systems, and they *should* have gone off. Should have been able to give them enough video evidence to identify the arsonist.

But, even more concerning than the lacking security at the motel, the security had been taken off-line, with Quinn being none the wiser. She was having her security guy look into it, and he had thought he might be able to find something, but until he did, it was another dead end.

It made Hawk jumpy. Fires were one thing, especially in some remote motel with uninterested employees. But someone who had the ability to bypass security systems and set three fires without being caught over the course of only a few days...

Something was very wrong.

Hawk glanced around, not realizing he was looking for Anna until he found her. She'd moved—he assumed she'd convinced Quinn to move with her, as Quinn was now sitting on a bench and had Pita in her lap. Clearly the other woman was taking some comfort in the dog. The boyfriend was hovering around her, and Hawk figured he'd look into Dunne Thompson too—but his gut feeling told him the guy was clean. Unless he was a hell of an actor, he was just as shocked at the security breach as Quinn was, if not more so.

All to get to Anna. Or scare her. It all connected to Anna and that meant...too many things to count. Particularly since there didn't seem to be any attempt at contacting Anna. No threats, warnings or ransom demands. Just...destruction.

Hawk finished up the necessary tasks, gave the last firemen a few more instructions, then briefly convened with Hart, all the while mentally preparing for the next step.

It was getting close to lunchtime. Anna needed food and rest. He needed to call the lab again, and a million other small tasks that would eventually lead to a suspect. But for now it felt frustratingly slow.

Especially knowing whoever had done this could hack into security systems. Hawk moved over to Anna and gave Quinn a few words of encouragement, told her he'd be in touch. He ushered Anna back to his truck.

"Call your brother," he instructed.

She wrinkled her nose at him. "Why?"

"Because whoever set this fire hacked into Quinn's impressive security. Which means the same could happen at Hudson Ranch. I want him to know to be on the lookout for the same."

He could see by her expression she had a million questions, but she surprised him. Instead of voicing them, she pulled her phone out of her pocket and explained everything he'd said to Palmer while he got Pita settled in the back.

Hawk looked around at their surroundings. Small Wyoming towns weren't usually hotbeds for criminal activity. Someone should have seen something—if not at the motel, then at his house or at the investigation office. Then again, Anna's investigating usually took place in Bent County, which meant that her targets were usually locals. They would know how to sneak around, he supposed. Hide in plain sight even.

But the lack of any threats prior to the murder attempt just didn't sit right. They were missing something. He gave her a sideways glance. Or *he* was missing something.

The fact of the matter was, he might think he had some…strange fundamental understanding of Anna Hudson, even if her family baffled him, but that didn't mean he knew the intricacies of her past.

"Anything you're not telling me, Blondie?"

She turned to look at him, and there was enough confusion on her face that he believed whatever they were missing, they were both missing it.

"What would I be keeping from you?" It bothered him that hurt was laced in her tone.

So he kept his gaze hard on the road in front of him. "I don't know. But I feel like I'm missing this big piece of something. It doesn't add up. A murder attempt out of nowhere, then these two petty scare tactics or warnings or whatever they are. It's backward."

"Maybe, but people sometimes are." She shrugged, and it poked at him she could be so casual about the whole thing.

"That's your grand philosophy as an investigator? Oh well, sometimes people are backward? Sometimes you just *don't* make sense of things?"

"Yeah, it is," she returned. And she didn't get all snarky like he expected, or poke at *his* investigative philosophy. She looked at him with soft eyes and spoke calmly. "Hawk, my parents disappeared into thin air when I was eight. Not only did the whole damn town look for them for way longer than made sense, but also I'd be willing to bet Jack has never actually stopped—though he claims he has. I can almost guarantee every one of us kids spent some time doing our own investigation over the past seventeen years. I know Palmer and I did. Hell, I bet even Mary did, and that's not her thing. My point is some things never make sense. Because the world doesn't have to."

She was right, which was annoying. An arson investigation was less about things like motivation, less about the *reasons*, and more about who started the fire and how.

The reason for the initial spark always had answers, and he'd always, always found them.

He couldn't let this case be the first time he didn't find out why. Any other case could be that. Not this one.

He drove out of Wilde, back toward Sunrise, chewing that frustration over. Hart had said he'd be out at the Hudson Ranch around one to ask the family questions. Hawk knew he'd wanted to talk to the family members individually, without Anna around, but Hawk wanted to hear, firsthand, what her family had to say.

He glanced at the clock. He should be able to get to the ranch right in time to walk in on something.

"Did you ever look for your dad?" she asked into the heavy quiet.

He froze, from the inside out. It was an unexpected question, and a painful wound he didn't want to discuss. Ever. With anyone.

But he had this underlying, secondary goal to everything he did with Anna. Because he was determined she marry him before their baby was born. *Because* of all those things he didn't like to talk about.

He didn't think the truth about his life made him sound like a particularly winning prize, but it would at least clarify why he wanted to be fully involved in his child's life. And that was all this was anyway. A surefire way to be a fully committed father.

So why not explain all the ways his hadn't been? "After my mom died, I became a ward of the state. They tried to find close relations, but there were none or they didn't want me. So I bounced around in foster homes till I aged out. When I did, I made it my mission to find my father, even if the system hadn't been able to. I thought I was going into it with my eyes wide open."

"Yeah," she said softly. "Don't we always at eighteen."

He laughed, and it didn't feel as bitter as it once had. Maybe because he wasn't eighteen anymore, and something about the way she said it fully crystallized the fact for him that no one would have been able to convince him not to do it. No one, not even his own mother if she'd lived, would have been able to talk him out of it.

Some lessons you had to learn on your own.

"I found him, felt pretty smug about that, too. I made it clear I didn't need anything from him—not anymore. I just wanted to give him a chance to make up for his screwup. For making it rougher on my mom than it needed to be, for the years of having to be the one to take care of her even though she didn't want me to. For those four years I'd been left with no one. I had it all planned out. I thought I had every scenario worked out in my head. Apologies, excuses, ignorance." Hawk didn't like to relive it, but it was right there. Like a movie playing in his head. "He looked me straight in the eye, said he didn't give a damn about me, or my mom, and never would. No remorse. No excuses. Just flat-out did not care."

Hawk focused on driving, but he felt Anna's gaze on him. She was quiet. Hell, even the puppy in the back was quiet. He'd spent a lot of years trying to treat that one moment like a learning experience: you never could predict the next moment in your life or what a person would do.

At eighteen, he hadn't been prepared for the cold callousness of his own father. All these years later, he understood there were a lot worse things to be. But that didn't ease or heal the hurt.

"You're telling me all this so I'll feel sorry for you and marry you," Anna said softly, surprising him.

Because if Anna wasn't evidence of that *life is unpredictable* lesson, he didn't know what was. She never did or said quite what he expected.

And he didn't hate it when it was her.

In this moment, specifically, because she was right on the money. And there was no point lying about it. "Mostly."

He pulled into the entrance of the Hudson Ranch. All centuries of roots and vast landscapes she belonged to. When he belonged to nothing and no one.

Except the child she carried.

"I can't say it's going to work, but I respect it as a solid tactic."

"Gee, thanks."

She flashed him a smile, and nothing about this woman made sense because in the midst of too many old memories, new problems and pressing danger, he smiled back.

ANNA STEPPED INTO the living room and immediately recoiled at the tension in the room. It was old, ugly and familiar. Even Pita stopped like he could feel it, too.

It was like stepping back in time. Cops in the house. Questions without answers. Worry and fear and no answers.

Except she wasn't a child any longer. In fact, was carrying what would become *her* child. And she knew this was not a future she wanted for her kid. Tension and questions that never got answered.

She looked at the source of it all—Thomas Hart—not that it was his fault. But he'd obviously been the question asker who had Cash looking furious and Izzy burrowed into his side with two of her puppies on her lap.

Anna had stopped at the threshold because of that wall of tension, but Izzy caught sight of her and jumped up and ran over to her. Anna was surprised by the exuberant greeting. No matter how much Anna enjoyed Izzy and vice versa, they saw each other too much for excited greetings.

"Terrorizing my family, Hart?" Anna said, smoothing a hand over Izzy's braid. It wasn't fair to lay any blame on his shoulders.

But she didn't really care about fair right now.

Hart shared an unreadable look with Hawk, then met Anna's accusatory gaze.

"I'm doing my job and investigating the attempted murder case. Part of that investigation requires me to ask a few questions of the people who know you well, who might be able to give us some leads on someone who might have wanted to kill you."

It was all calm, almost even pleasantly stated. But Anna knew too many cops. How they thought. What they meant. She'd give Hart credit for being able to put a nice little mask on all that.

But *wanted to kill you* was meant to put her in her place.

"Ms. Hudson, I was hoping to question each of your family members alone. It's best if they're not influenced by worrying over your feelings. You're an investigator. You understand."

She hated that he was using that tactic, but she also knew she'd do the same in his shoes. "Yeah, I understand."

"Steele, why don't you—"

"I'm going to be in the room. It's my investigation, too." Hart's mouth firmed, but he didn't mount an argument. Which, of course, left room for Cash to stand and mount one. "Izzy's done. You want to go another few rounds with me? Fine. But my daughter is leaving with Anna."

"Mr. Hudson, this isn't an interrogation," Hart said gently. "We're simply trying to—"

"I know what you're trying to do. She's *eleven*. She's done." Cash gave Anna a nod, and though Anna wanted to argue at being ordered around, she also wanted to get Izzy out of this ugly situation Anna had been in more times than she could count.

Anna turned, a hand on Izzy's shoulder, but Izzy hesitated.

"What about my mom?" she whispered up at Anna. But it clearly wasn't enough of a whisper. Anna felt Hawk tense next to her. But Hart didn't hear it, and it didn't appear Cash did either, so Anna just kept moving Izzy toward the kitchen, tugging Pita behind her on his leash.

Leaving the men behind, her heart beating heavy in her chest. She didn't dare look back at Hawk.

She hadn't thought of that little altercation with Chessa around Christmas. It couldn't have anything to do with this, so it just… It hadn't even been a thought.

Hawk would no doubt think she had been purposefully keeping something from him. It shouldn't matter to her if she had or not. Family came first.

Not Hawk Steele.

But she *hadn't* been hiding. She hadn't thought of it as possibly connecting. It couldn't connect.

She tried to tell herself that as she crouched so she could be eye to eye with Izzy, though it didn't take much crouching these days. The girl was growing like a weed.

"Izzy, that thing with your mom…" Anna didn't know how to explain it. None of this was fair, but she'd been in an unfair situation when she'd been younger than Izzy. She tried to treat Izzy like she would have wanted to be treated then.

"I didn't want to say anything in front of Dad," Izzy said, blue eyes filling with tears. "He gets so upset when I talk about Mom. I know he doesn't want me to see it, but I see it. And I just… The detective asked about people who'd hurt you, and I know Mom hurt you, Aunt Anna. I just…"

"I know." And she hated that Izzy was keeping a secret, but… It would kill Cash. That Chessa had been sneaking around the ranch, trying to find Izzy. That Anna was pretty sure she'd been high on something when she'd almost, *almost* gotten her hands on Izzy. "If I'd thought of…" Anna shook her head. It didn't matter what she'd thought of. "That thing with your mom has nothing to do with this. It was a real smart line of thinking, though. I'm impressed. It didn't even occur to me." Anna tried to smile encouragingly. "But you don't need to worry about that. What we're dealing with isn't about your mom, or her and me fighting."

Which was what adults had said to her for years after her parents had disappeared. *You don't need to worry about that.* Back then, it had made her so mad. Now she understood why the adults in her life had been frustrating. Danger and confusion were no places for a kid.

Before Anna could think of something better to say, Cash stormed out. It was a carefully contained storm, but it was all thunder and lightning nonetheless.

And Anna felt…guilty. Even though this particular situation wasn't her fault. There was that old situation she'd kept from him and…

"Cash—"

"I don't want to hear an apology from you, Anna. This isn't your fault. Someone tried to…" His gaze darted to his daughter. "…hurt you. We need to get to the bottom of it. My frustration over how that cop handled it isn't on you." He moved over to Izzy, ran his hand over her braid. "Or you, sweetheart."

Izzy smiled up at him, but it was wobbly. Anna felt wobbly herself. Because Hawk wasn't going to let this line of questioning go, and it was going to hurt Cash beyond measure.

And it put them no closer to figuring out who wanted her dead.

Chapter Ten

Hawk sat through the rest of the questions with Anna's family. He asked a few of his own. No one said anything of any note. Louisa had noted the tire slashing story from high school Anna had already told him. Mary had mentioned a cold case client who'd asked Anna out and been politely refused a few years back. Palmer had a few names from the rodeo of men Anna had rebuffed, but thought it was a bad thread to tug since none of the men had pressed the issue.

They didn't get a chance to talk with Jack, but Hart said he'd make an appointment at the Sunrise sheriff's office tomorrow morning that Hawk could attend.

Maybe had demanded to attend.

"You're kind of overstepping your bounds, don't you think?" Hart asked, sounding almost casual as he slid his pen and notebook into his pocket.

So Hawk maintained the fake casualness and didn't tense or shoot back the words piling up in his throat. He kept his voice deceptively mild. "My bounds are figuring out who started that fire, same as yours are to figure out who wants her dead."

"Yeah," Hart agreed. It seemed like he was going to voice a "but" but he never did. "I'll see you in the morning."

"Yeah." Hawk didn't offer to walk Hart out. He didn't offer a goodbye. He just turned and left the room.

He needed to find Anna. Because Izzy had said something to her, and Hawk needed to find out what. Needed to understand what secret she was keeping from him.

He couldn't delve into why he was keeping that little piece of information from Hart. It was silly and probably put Anna in extra danger. Hart should share every piece of information there was, just like Hawk. Two sets of eyes, two investigators, were better than one.

But no amount of rational thinking changed Hawk's course of action, because he knew Anna would be hurt by him telling Hart and he just…couldn't.

Anna wasn't in the kitchen with Mary and Izzy. She wasn't in her room, which was empty. It still wasn't quite dinnertime yet, so the Hudson clan was scattered hither and yon doing whatever a cold case investigative business did.

He looked through the whole house and didn't find her. He stepped outside. It was too damn cold for her to be gallivanting out around the ranch. And she was nowhere to be seen in the front.

Just about when his nerves were pulling tight enough to snap, he heard something. More from the back of the house, but still outside. He followed the wraparound porch all the way back to where there was a porch swing.

Anna and Palmer sat on it, chatting and laughing as it swung gently. Anna had a thick coat on—one he was pretty sure was Palmer's—and a blanket tucked around her.

No doubt Palmer was sitting with her because she shouldn't be alone, and because it was damn cold, but there was also a genuine contentment there. Brother and sister, happily enjoying each other's company.

Because she was always taken care of here—the Hudsons took care of one another. With or without parents. Anna certainly didn't need Hawk's help with anything, and neither would their kid. That was clear.

It was a painful, terrifying thought. One he couldn't sit with because Anna looked over as if sensing him here.

Palmer looked over too, then slid off the swing. "Well. This feels a little too third wheel for me." He walked past Hawk and gave him a little nudge toward Anna.

As if Hawk needed one. He walked over, though he didn't sit. Because Anna's gaze was firmly out on the mountains in the distance. Not him.

Her roots. Her family. This life she had that was perfectly capable—and willing—to do anything for a kid who wasn't even here yet.

"Where's my dog?" he offered, hoping his voice didn't sound as affected as it felt.

"Cash was having a training session with the other puppies, so I figured Pita could use some sibling time. And some work on following orders."

"That he could." Hawk stood there and waited. And waited. Because he could feel the tension coiling into her. Guilt. Finally she visibly swallowed and slowly brought her gaze from the mountains to him.

He'd expected some kind of challenge. A self-righteous determination she was right to keep something from him. Lectures. Maybe he even expected her to use that heat between them to distract him from the topic at hand.

Which might have worked, he hated to admit.

Instead, she looked like she was about to cry. "Hawk,

whatever you think you heard, I promise you—it has nothing to do with someone trying to kill me."

He felt twin pangs—anger that she would just make that determination without explaining anything to him, and the desperate need to stop her from looking so heartbreakingly sad.

He decided to hold on to anger, best he could. It felt safer. "Well, how about I be the judge of that, since you didn't want to share it with the police officer investigating the *attempted murder* on you."

"Hawk."

"You said you weren't keeping anything from me."

"And I'm not. This was nothing. It was family stuff. It never *occurred* to me it might connect. I promise." She seemed so desperate for him to believe her. Like it mattered that she kept his trust.

And that it did…mattered to him.

Hell, he was screwed. He took the seat Palmer had vacated, rested his elbows on his knees and looked out at those majestic peaks. He kept his feet firmly planted on the ground, though. No swinging for him. He'd tried to build himself into one of those mountains—strong and immovable. If he looked at her, he was sure he'd crumble.

"This would kill Cash. Just gut him," Anna said quietly. Quiet enough he felt compelled to look and risk that crumble.

"I'm not Cash, Anna. I'm not asking you to tell Cash. I'm asking you to tell *me*. For the investigation. If nothing else, it's another name I can cross off the list."

"Chessa's name wasn't on the list to begin with."

But he knew that name because Hawk had made sure to know *all* the players. "So this is about Cash's ex-wife?"

She blew out a breath and looked away again. "Nothing is about Chessa, because the whole…thing Izzy was talking about happened years ago. It doesn't relate."

"How many years?"

She swallowed, eyes big and swimming with hurt as she expressly did not make eye contact. "Last…year."

Hawk swore and nearly got up off the swing, but Anna grasped his arm.

"She was lurking around the ranch. I happened to be the one who found her. She said she wanted to see Izzy, was trying to get her hands on Izzy. I told her to beat it. She got a little…handsy. But she's just not… It's not like she had a weapon. She was maybe high and tried to punch me. I dodged, gave her a good knock, but—"

"So you got into a physical fight with someone, *less* than a year ago, who was unstable and potentially on drugs, and it didn't occur to you that it might connect?"

She shook her head, and damn it, one of those tears slipped over. "No, it didn't."

The worst part was, he believed her. No matter what kind of fool that made him. "We cannot ignore that kind of possibility. I have to at the very least look into her."

"It doesn't make sense. Why would she want to hurt *me*? She knows any one of us would stop her from getting her hands on Izzy. Cash most of all, so it's not… It wouldn't be personal to me."

"You don't think she'd hurt you to hurt Cash?"

Anna blinked, again as if the thought hadn't occurred to her. "That… It wouldn't make sense. There are better targets than me. Izzy chief among them."

"You were literally lecturing me a few hours ago on

how things didn't make sense and backward things are sometimes just backward."

She sighed, closing her eyes and leaning her head against the swing's back. "Do you have to remember everything?"

"Comes with the territory."

She blew out a breath. "Is there a way to make sure Cash doesn't know Chessa is in the mix?"

"I'll do everything I can."

She turned to him, wrapped her arms around him and squeezed. "Thank you." She pulled back and studied him. "Not sure I would have pegged you for such a good guy, Hawk."

"I think I'll take that as a compliment."

She smiled, her arms still draped over his shoulders. She was so beautiful it made him ache. "This is something, Blondie. I don't know what, but it isn't just because of the kid."

She was quiet for a long moment, studying him with those hazel eyes. He didn't know what she was looking for, what she saw, but she swallowed. "Isn't it?" she asked on a whisper.

"No." No, because it had been like this from the first. And just like the first, he couldn't think from wanting her. So he leaned forward and kissed her. And just like the first time, it was a bolt that made everything else disappear. All that existed in this world was them. The way she tasted like something dark and decadent, but her arms around him felt like sunlight after a long, hard winter.

Someone cleared their throat. Once, maybe twice. It took Hawk a few moments to fully engage with sounds other than the little world of kissing they'd created for themselves.

He managed to move his head away from her and look toward the noise.

Jack Hudson stood there looking like any father of a teenage daughter might in finding said daughter wrapped up in the arms of the town juvenile delinquent.

Too bad they were all adults, and Jack wasn't anyone's father.

"Dinner is ready," he said flatly. "And we have some things to discuss."

"Did you want to grill him on his intentions?" Anna asked, sliding off the swing and throwing the blanket over her shoulder. Hawk followed her over to where Jack stood and figured he might as well start expanding his campaign.

"Please do. I've already told her she should marry me, but she's being stubborn about it."

Jack opened his mouth. Closed it. Then opened and closed it again. All without making a sound.

"Aw, look. You made him speechless," Anna said, grinning as they walked past Jack. "Major points, Hawk."

"Might have to hold you to this point system."

And she laughed. That bawdy, reckless laugh of hers that seemed to crawl inside of him and change everything. And she took his hand, lacing her fingers with his, changing whatever was left.

ANNA FELT ALL warm and fuzzy. She supposed maybe she should feel guilty about that, in the midst of all this ugly stuff, but if there was anything her childhood taught her it was that tragedy and grief went together with joy and love. Good things happened during bad times and vice versa.

As she walked inside, holding hands with Hawk, she

put her free hand over her stomach, wondering if the baby growing in there had any idea how much it was loved. Before it was even here. That was a blessing.

Unfortunately, she was definitely not doing a very good job of proving to Hawk she'd make a bad wife, but maybe… Maybe she wouldn't. Maybe…somehow, improbably, they just…worked.

The thought made her nervous, so she pushed it away. Determined to enjoy family dinner, with Hawk by her side.

The warm, fuzzy feeling lasted for all of five minutes. Because that was all it took to have everyone gathered around the table, Pita happily snoozing at Hawk's feet, and Jack taking the lead. Not talking about ranch things or HSS things or even Sunrise things.

"With the lack of movement in the case, Hart wanted the files for all the cold cases Anna's worked on with HSS," Jack said, passing the bowl of rolls over to Grant. "I can't do that, obviously. Much like Fool's Gold, it skirts the boundaries of privacy. However, that's not any reason to let someone keep coming after Anna."

Anna looked down at the food on her plate. She tried to pretend this was any joint HSS case, but how could she just ignore the fact she was at the center of all of it? And her family and Hawk and Hart and probably a million other people were poking through her life, determining who might hate her enough to kill.

It was exhausting.

"Mary's already started organizing the files and will finish after dinner. We'll split them up, go over anything Anna even remotely touched. We'll look through and consider any angry parties. None stick out to me from memory, so this might be a waste of time, but—"

"Nothing is a waste of time in an investigation," Hawk finished for him.

Jack nodded, a change from the disapproval—and then shock—outside.

"Obviously, we're looking for injured parties," Jack continued. "People who feel they might have been wronged, which of course doesn't mean anyone actually *was*." He looked pointedly in her direction, like she needed to hear it.

But she wasn't Mary. She wasn't a blame-yourself-for-the-ridiculousness-of-others type of girl.

"Hawk, do you have anything to add?" Jack asked.

And it was a strange tableau. Loaded plates. Her whole family. Every single head swiveling to look down at Hawk. Except Anna herself.

She could only stare at her brother. Who asked for opinions and input about once an epoch. Now he was asking... Hawk?

"The thing that connects these incidents is Anna and fire. *Anything* that might hint at arson should also be some kind of clue. So even if there isn't a clear case of potential blame, even a hint of fire gets added to the list."

There was a murmur of assent and agreement, a few more comments as they ate. Then slowly the chatter moved toward less serious things. The upcoming springtime calving and Izzy's teacher's latest antics in trying to control the class and even a progress report on Pita's training. It was all very normal and should have lifted her spirits.

But pregnancy exhaustion plagued Anna, as did the idea that they could sit around and act like everything was normal, but it *wasn't*. Because everyone was going to be poring over old files, determining who she might have made angry enough to want her dead.

After dinner, Anna made the excuse that she was tired and left them to it. She didn't want to look at old files. She didn't want to be in the room where all her mistakes were paraded out like a list of facts suitable for an investigation.

She just went up to her room and crawled into bed and tried to fall asleep. But all she did was stare at the wall, feeling weirdly weepy and refusing to cry, while she thought of everyone she'd been not so nice to in her whole damn life.

And now her family was down there, discussing, dissecting and sharing it with Hawk. And it just felt *gross*.

When the door creaked open, she stiffened and closed her eyes without fully thinking the move through. She just…didn't want to face him. Or anyone. She wanted to… Well, if she was being honest with herself, she wanted to wallow in how much she sucked.

Hawk was very careful and quiet. She heard the faint rustle of clothes being changed, but almost nothing else. The bed dipped as he slid into it and she kept her eyes carefully closed, hoping he'd just…go to bed. She felt too soft and vulnerable to talk to anyone, let alone him.

But his arms came around her, and he pulled her close. "All right, Blondie, what's bothering you?"

She didn't know why she liked that nickname. She was sure she should be offended that it relegated her to a body part, but it had become…theirs somehow. And the way he said it, all warm or disapproving or in that sexy growl, it…meant something. He wasn't a nickname type guy. It made her feel special.

"Oh, Hawk, what could possibly be bothering me?"

He chuckled, resting his chin on her shoulder. She'd noticed he'd been very careful about touching her stomach. He almost never did it, which was a little strange considering he was ready to get married over what was growing there.

But carefully, gingerly, his hands moved over her abdomen and linked there, over the baby they'd created that she was working to grow.

She wanted to cry at that alone.

"Something about dinner, specifically, is bothering you," he said into her ear.

There was something…special about him noticing that. Sure, he was an investigator and maybe it was just an offshoot of that, but for all he didn't know about her, he seemed to…understand pieces of her. She'd had a few serious boyfriends. Well, maybe *serious* wasn't the right word. *Long-term* seemed better suited.

None of them had ever understood her changes in mood. Or tried to. She really couldn't fathom just agreeing to marry Hawk when she only knew bits and pieces about him. Louisa wasn't rushing to marry Palmer when she'd known him practically her whole life.

But they also weren't having a baby, she supposed.

And thinking about all that was better than thinking about what was really bothering her. She knew she could distract Hawk with sex, but she also knew he'd just bring it up again later. It would only be a temporary reprieve.

"Anna," he said, bringing her back to the present.

"I don't know how to explain it, exactly. It's just this weird… I don't like everyone poking around in everything I've ever done. I get why we have to do it, and when it was my work with Quinn, or even my old boyfriends…that didn't get under my skin. But this is… This is my family trying to determine all the ways someone I've come into contact with might hate me. And it isn't just my life out there. It's about how I've handled cases with our family business." She stumbled over the next words, even though once upon a time she would have announced them loudly, brashly, proudly. She didn't feel very proud right now. "I... I've never been a very nice person."

"Join the club, Anna."

She turned in the circle of his arms, so she could look at him. Or impress upon him that... "But you're a good guy," she said, touching his cheek with her palm.

"And you're a good...gal?"

She snorted.

"Neither of us are perfect, but I think we both have a pretty good sense of right and wrong and wanting to do the right thing. It's why we do the jobs we do." He tucked a strand of hair behind her ear in a soft, loving gesture. "And regardless, even if you were the absolute worst person in the world, I'm pretty sure that family of yours would love you anyway."

Love. She looked at his face, shadowed in the dark, and wondered why that word should stick out. When of course her family loved her. She'd always, *always* been surrounded by love.

He hadn't.

She found herself wanting to be the person who gave him that. What her family had given her. A soft place to land. Joy. Teamwork.

And yet... She didn't know how to just...accept that. Jump into this whole unknown existence. Particularly when someone was trying to kill her in this one. "You guys didn't find anything, did you?"

"Not tonight, but there are still cases to get through."

He kept holding her there, gently. Because he wanted to protect her from all this ugliness, but she could read him a little too well. The way he tried to shield her. It just wasn't all that different from the ways her family had tried to shield her most of her childhood.

And it *was* born out of care, so she didn't find herself getting angry. Just resigned. She rested her forehead between his shoulder and his jaw. "You think there's going to be another fire, don't you?"

He sighed, the breath ruffling her hair. "It seems unlikely they'd stop."

Motel, her truck, her work. She knew what those kinds of patterns meant. "I don't want it to be here."

"I know."

"You think it will be."

He was quiet for a long time, but he didn't lie to her. He held her tighter. "Yeah, I do."

"So do I."

He tucked her closer into his body, a more comfortable position for sleep. "We've got a lot of security. All we can do tonight is get some rest, so we're ready to face whatever tomorrow brings. We're going to get to the bottom of this. I won't rest until we do."

She knew that was a promise he intended to keep, but she knew that sometimes…there was no getting to the bottom of it. Sometimes promises were made and not kept.

But she didn't have the heart to tell him that.

Chapter Eleven

Hawk woke up in the dark to the bed shaking and the sound of muffled sobs filling up the room.

Did she do this every night? It damn near tore him in half. "Anna." He gave her a gentle little shake. But she just kept crying. Eyes closed, fast asleep.

It absolutely broke his heart. So he kept giving her gentle little nudges and desperately trying to get through to her. "Anna. Anna. Come on, Blondie. Wake up."

She blinked her eyes open. The dark clearly confused her, but when she turned her head to look at him in the shadows, she seemed to understand.

She lifted her hands to her face and touched the tears there. "Oh."

Just *oh*. Like this was commonplace for her and…well, clearly it was. He didn't think it was just a pregnancy thing, as she'd said before, because she hadn't been pregnant long enough to make *sobbing* in your sleep commonplace.

"Anna."

She shook her head. "It's nothing. Not really. Just happens sometimes."

"Define *sometimes*."

She sighed, exhausted, and he wanted to let her go back to sleep, but…this was like some terrifying unknown he couldn't fix for her. Which felt a little too on the nose considering he also couldn't seem to fix the whole someone-wanting-to-kill-her thing, even when it was his job.

"I'm not sure what causes it. I never remember if it's a dream or… I just wake up and my face is wet and I'm crying. It started after my parents disappeared. I thought I'd grown out of it."

He knew all too well what it felt like to be a child and powerless without your parents. Maybe she'd had a lot more family than he had, but he didn't think it changed it. Sometimes, you just wanted your mother.

And sometimes, she just couldn't be there.

"When did you realize you hadn't?" he asked gently, pulling her close and stroking her hair.

"You said I'd done it the other night."

Stress, clearly. Didn't take a psychologist to figure that out. But it killed him he couldn't take away that anxiety for her.

A knock sounded on the door, and they both swung toward the noise, fighting stances at the ready. Even though a threat wouldn't knock.

"Stay right there," he muttered, sliding out of bed. He opened the door to the hallway light on and Palmer looking grim.

"We've got a situation."

"What kind of situation?" Anna demanded from where she was still sitting in bed.

"You stay put," Palmer said.

"I will not—"

"I don't want her alone," Hawk interrupted, hoping to avoid sibling arguments until he knew what this was. He didn't think it was that fire he was afraid of or there'd be more urgency. "Is Mary up?"

Palmer nodded. "Yeah. I'll walk with Anna down the hall, fill Mary in. Jack is downstairs. He can get you up to speed."

"How about *you* fill *me* in?" Anna demanded of Palmer, coming to stand next to Hawk. Her hair was disheveled, but she'd at least wiped up all trace of tears. Though Palmer did stare at her face for a shade too long.

Hawk pressed a kiss to her temple. "We'll tell you everything, I promise. But right now, you're the target. You stay safe." He placed his hand over her stomach, something he'd been avoiding doing because... Well, for a lot of reasons. Mostly that the idea of a kid jangled up inside of him in a million different knots. He could know he had a responsibility to be a father, know how he wanted that to look.

It didn't mean he knew how to *deal*.

"Your job is to keep you both safe," Hawk said, trying to sound firm instead of strangled.

And he knew he got her there because her expression changed. She nodded and walked with Palmer down the hall while Hawk took the stairs and found Jack.

Jack gestured him into the security room. "Palmer talked to Landon Thompson, the guy who set up Quinn Peterson's security. The computer jargon is over my head, but Palmer thinks there might have been a security breach tonight based on what Landon told him. Know anything about this stuff?"

Hawk surveyed the computers with some irritation. "Not as much as I'd need to."

"Luckily Palmer does," Jack said, and Hawk wished he could find some comfort in that, but he wanted to know what to look for. How to fix this. But all he saw was a maze of monitors and screens and cords.

He did better with facts and names and evidence. The wreckage of fire. Or had, until this impossible case.

"If you married her—" Jack began.

But Hawk was in no mood. "That'd be our business."

"Sure," Jack agreed, far too easily. "Doesn't change the fact that if you hurt her, I'd be forced to kill you and make sure you were a cold case that never got investigated. Married or no."

"Color me unsurprised." Hawk moved his gaze from the monitors to Jack. "Or undeterred."

Jack gave him a nod, like he had tonight at the dinner table. Hawk was hesitant to call it approval, but it wasn't *disapproval*.

"Good."

Hawk found himself oddly…moved by that. He'd long ago learned to live without the approval of anyone. He did what he did for himself, and for the memory of his mother. Nothing and no one else.

But suddenly earning Jack's approval felt important. It would matter to Anna—no matter how much she might try to say it didn't. So it mattered to him.

"Are we threatening him?" Palmer asked, striding into the small room—a room definitely too small for three large men, but they huddled in. Because they had to figure out how to analyze this threat.

"Yeah," Jack replied casually.

"Death or torture?"

"I figured I'd handle death."

"Cool. I'll take torture." Palmer grinned at Hawk. "I'm great at torture."

Hawk understood that it was both a joke and some-what serious all at the same time. A warning. The Hud-sons were a unit, and he was interfering in that unit. But the smile, the teamwork, well, it was a tentative truce and acceptance that they'd work together to keep Anna safe.

And if Hawk always did, they wouldn't have any prob-lems.

"But for now…" Palmer pointed at the computers. "There was a glitch. Just like Landon explained happened in the Fool's Gold security. But I can't get to the source of it or undo it. It's complicated and high-tech. Landon still hadn't gotten to the bottom of it, and I got the feeling he had more skills than I did. The problem is, while we're try-ing to figure that out, we can't trust what we see up here," he said, pointing to the monitors.

Hawk definitely didn't like the idea they couldn't trust the surveillance. That was the whole point of staying here.

"I have a feeling the next step is another fire," Hawk said, taking in what part of the ranch each monitor showed. "Here. It started with the murder attempt, then it was her truck, then it was her place of work. Home is the next rea-sonable target. So, if something went wrong with the sur-veillance equipment tonight specifically, I think we need to look out for the chance of fire tonight. Specifically."

He glanced at the two men, who looked grim and yet unsurprised.

"We'll need to wake up Cash, get Izzy over here. Wak-ing everyone up would be best," Jack said. "All hands on deck."

"It's a big spread. Lots of places to start fires, but it won't be random," Hawk said. The problem was, it all meant something to Anna, it all threatened her or someone she loved, so there were a lot of options. "It'll be some-where that might hurt. So, yeah. All hands on deck."

And as if he'd spoken it into the ether, a dog began to bark. Pita. Somewhere outside, another one began to howl.

None of the men said anything. They just started run-ning.

ANNA PACED MARY'S ROOM. She couldn't settle because Palmer's explanation of the problem had made her nerves hum. She also couldn't settle because Mary's room was like a shrine to orderliness and cleanliness—and freakishly white. Anna was always afraid she'd mess something up.

And, okay, sometimes she messed something up on purpose. But not tonight. Tonight…

"Anna, you're making me dizzy," Mary said in exas-peration. She was sitting at her prim little *white* desk, care-fully going through case files.

"I just don't know why I couldn't go down and look at the computers like Palmer."

"Well, you could," Mary said calmly, placing one file neatly on the other, then looking up at Anna. "As I have never once in your entire life known you to follow an order."

Anna scowled, because it was true. Because she *should* just march down there and demand to be involved.

But didn't, because Hawk had put his hand on her stom-ach, where some baby the size of a peach grew, completely unaware of everything going on around them.

Mary turned in her chair and studied Anna. "I've never seen you like this."

"Well, I've never been pregnant before," Anna grum-bled, even knowing that wasn't what Mary meant. Even knowing the way she was acting had to do with Hawk as much as pregnancy.

"So, that's the only explanation for how you are around Hawk?" Mary said, in that careful way that strangers thought meant she was agreeing with them.

She never was.

"And how am I around Hawk?"

Mary took a minute to consider. Then smiled. "Thunderstruck."

Anna recoiled. "I do *not* think so."

"If it makes you feel better, he's equally thunderstruck by you." She turned back to her desk like this was all just normal conversation. And obvious. When surely...

Well, maybe he was a *little* something-struck by her. It shouldn't—she really didn't want it to—but it did make her feel better. The idea of making Hawk Steele thunderstruck, well, it was a powerful feeling and—

She heard the faint yip of a dog. Pita, no doubt. She should go downstairs and—

Then, outside and farther away, the howling of another dog. One of the older dogs that would be over by Cash's cabin. Anna looked over at Mary, who was already on her feet.

"You should stay here," Mary said. "I'll go see—"

Anna crossed and grabbed her sister's arm. "We're going together. No one goes it alone, right? Did Louisa stay? We should grab her too, if Palmer's downstairs already."

Mary hesitated, but only for a moment before she nodded. "All right. Let's get her."

Louisa was already out in the hall when they stepped out. So were Grant and Dahlia. Grant was carrying two guns.

"We don't know what's going on just yet, but the dogs

sense something and the security has been tampered with." He handed one gun to Louisa. "You're coming with me." He looked over at Anna. "You three are staying put."

Anna opened her mouth to argue, rote habit, but Grant shook his head. Still, he handed her the other gun in his hand.

"I know you don't like holding back, but Dahlia hates guns almost as much as Mary does. I know you can handle yourself with one should the need arise, so I'd appreciate it if you stayed back."

Mary and Dahlia might hate guns, but they both knew how to shoot. She scowled at her brother. "You're full of it, Grant Hudson."

His mouth *almost* curved ruefully. "Not completely. It's a solid plan even if you don't like it. We'll send Izzy up when we can. It's possible this is all a…false alarm."

"Don't placate us, Grant," Dahlia said disapprovingly.

He leaned forward and placed a kiss on his girlfriend's cheek. "We'll be back. Keep your phones on you."

Then Grant and Louisa disappeared downstairs, and Anna stood in the hallway with Mary and Dahlia and tried not to feel like some damsel in distress locked in a tower.

"There's plenty we can do," Mary said. "Just because you're used to doing the active work doesn't mean the groundwork isn't just as important. We have case files, and you have some computer expertise."

"Not as much as Palmer."

"Maybe not, but that doesn't mean you couldn't figure it out with time. I'll grab my files, and we'll go down to the surveillance room. It's as safe down there as it is up here."

Anna realized with a little start that she sometimes, in-advertently, underestimated her sister on *this* level. She knew Mary was the heart of how everything ran at both the ranch and HSS. She was the organizer, the analyzer, the details person. And it was easy to forget that because she did it all quietly, in the background. Without ever asking for help, attention or recognition.

Anna nodded, because her sister was right. There was still a lot to be done on this side of things. "Okay, yeah. That's a good plan."

Mary bustled back into her room to collect the files while Anna and Dahlia stood, as if frozen by circumstance.

"It'll be okay," Dahlia offered reassuringly. "Maybe this could even be the end of it," she offered hopefully.

Anna wanted to believe it could be, but it was a big ranch. So many places to hide, so many ways someone could get hurt.

So many ways to disappear.

She swallowed down that ugly thought and forced herself to smile at Dahlia. "Yeah, maybe it'll all be over."

Chapter Twelve

Hawk crept through the dark night, Pita by his side. He'd convinced Jack that a dog was enough of a partner until Cash and one of his dogs could meet up with him once he'd gotten Izzy tucked away in the house.

Which had put him on house duty, while Jack and Grant went to check on the animals together.

So Hawk moved around the house in slowly bigger circles. He listened. He searched for signs of someone. Hawk didn't see or smell signs of any fire, and it ate at him. Because he knew in his bones it was coming…just not exactly where. Or how.

He made another circle around the house. Anna was the target. She'd been the one who'd been hurt and left to die. The following fires being at her work and her truck meant the focus was on her.

But Hawk couldn't ignore the possibility that someone would hurt her family to hurt her. And if Jack or Grant got themselves hurt or worse out there, it would just feel like his fault. Like he'd let her down.

The thought ate him up inside.

He had to stop letting Anna be a distraction. He should be working night and day on this, not having family dinners and spending the night in her bed actually sleeping and not doing any work. He needed to—

Pita began to growl—something he'd never once heard the puppy do. Hawk crouched, wrapped his arm around the dog. Hawk didn't want him bounding off into the unknown.

He watched the shadows and tried to listen for something. The wind blew softly and cold. There was the odd rustle—but it could have been animal, the line of evergreen trees or even just the wind blowing snow around.

But Pita's growling didn't stop.

Hawk adjusted his grip on his gun. He had a flashlight, but he wasn't going to use it just yet. He also wasn't going to risk his dog.

Pita was vibrating in his arms—Hawk wasn't sure if it was fear or pent-up energy ready to attack. Either way...

"Stay," he said firmly to the dog. If Hawk had brought a leash with him, he would have tied Pita up, but as it was he just had to hope the commands they'd been working on worked. "Stay," he repeated.

Then he moved forward. Into the dark. Toward the sense of noise and shadow. He kept his peripheral vision on the house. Most of the lights were off, but Mary's bedroom was on this side, so a very dim light shone through the curtains there. It gave him enough of a sense that he would be able to see if someone tried to creep toward the house in the otherwise dark yard.

He willed Cash to hurry up because a bad feeling was crawling up his spine. Obviously, things were wrong, but something felt especially off.

Anna telling him sometimes people were backward kept echoing in his head. Reminding him you couldn't always reason bad choices and soulless people. Patterns didn't always have to make sense to the sane.

He gripped the flashlight and looked back at the dog. Pita was whimpering but staying. "Good dog," Hawk whispered. Cash would take the dog inside once he got here. Get him out of harm's way. So Pita just had to stay put for a few more minutes.

Please only be a few more minutes. The dog was too much of a distraction, a worry.

Hawk crept farther away from the house, trying to put Pita out of his mind. Whoever was after Anna was likely after starting a fire, not hurting a dog.

Hawk stilled and listened, trying to get a sense of what was out here—not worry about Pita and Anna. He'd never felt this torn before. Investigations and danger were easy.

Because he'd had no one and nothing for far too long. Now he had a…family. Weird and complicated and certainly not set in stone, but people and an animal he cared about. Needed to save and protect. Something he hadn't had to worry about since he was fourteen years old.

And look how that turned out.

Hawk shook that thought away. He hadn't been able to save his mother because she'd been *sick*. He'd damn well save Anna from some lunatic who wanted to hurt her. It was his job. Everything he'd built himself into. His very identity. Finding answers and stopping people from doing more harm.

But his heart thundered in his chest, and worry slithered into and scattered his focus. He'd never once had to do his job when he cared this much about the person he was protecting. He'd never dreamed he'd have to.

He heard two things at once—a shuffle, and Pita letting out a pained yelp. Instinct told him to move toward the shuffle sound for his own good, but he couldn't stand the thought of someone hurting Pita, so he turned toward the dog.

Mistake, he realized as pain bloomed out from the base of his skull…and turned his world dark.

"WHAT ABOUT THIS?" Dahlia said, pointing to the file she'd been reading. Anna had dozed off a little, not even getting through one file. She would have thought nerves and worry and frustration would have kept her wired and awake, but apparently not. She could only chalk it up to pregnancy, yet again.

Anna looked down at the keyboard she'd fallen asleep on. She hadn't gotten very far in trying to find the source of the glitch. Some help she was. She swiveled in her chair to try to focus on what Mary and Dahlia had found.

Izzy was curled up in a little nest of blankets in the corner with a puppy, both asleep and snoring lightly. Anna couldn't help but smile at the image they made. And the knowledge she was growing one of those. If everything went the way it should, someday she would have a son or daughter, curled into the corners of the Hudson Ranch… even if danger rained down around them.

She thought of Hawk as a boy, trying to take care of his dying mother. Being left alone. Being told he wasn't wanted by his own father. She wanted this family for him as much as she wanted it for their child.

But now was not the time for these thoughts. Because Hawk was outside, in the dark of night, heading off danger with her brothers and her best friend.

"This HSS client from a few years back," Dahlia was

saying to Mary. "He owned a computer company. Wouldn't that mean you know a lot about computers and how to hack into security systems?"

"Maybe," Mary agreed. "This was a client?" Mary asked, frowning as she moved over to Dahlia to look at the file. "Oh, yes. I remember this. A missing wife." She frowned. "But this was when Anna was in the rodeo. I don't think she would have worked any of it."

Both women looked over at her. Dahlia held out the case file for her to read.

Anna studied the information. "No, I didn't work on that case." But there was something familiar about the name of the victim. She tapped the page. "Francine Evans. Why does that sound familiar?" she mused aloud.

"I'm not sure. You might have heard us discuss it. One of the few cases we've ever taken where the missing person was still alive—and had changed her identity on purpose."

"To get away from her husband?" Dahlia asked.

"Sort of. She drained his bank accounts before she took off. He didn't *tell* us that, so it became a whole big complication. When we found her, she acted like she was afraid of her husband. When we told him we'd found her, but refused to tell him any details, he told us about the bank account and was angry we wouldn't help him. Basically, they both did a lot of lying, so in the end, we just pulled out of the whole mess. Told him to have the police handle it."

"So he might be angry with HSS," Dahlia said.

"Yes, but again, Anna wasn't here for that. She didn't work on the case. So why target her?"

"Who was the lead on this case? Cash?" Anna asked,

flipping pages. "If I was in the rodeo, Jack was just starting as sheriff, Grant was deployed, Palmer was with me. Cash and you were kind of holding down the fort, though Jack would have helped. And I guess Palmer and I might have stepped in during breaks, but I don't remember this one."

Anna looked back down at the file, and she flipped through it. Cash had indeed been the lead, and there wasn't any piece of this case that was familiar except a vague memory of Cash and Mary relaying the story.

But something about a computer company definitely felt like too much of a coincidence. The husband in this case was Clarence Samuels. He owned CS Computer Systems.

A name that was familiar to Anna for completely different reasons. "The guy I was following for Fool's Gold the day someone first tried to kill me? He was a salesman for CS Computer Systems. The same company this guy owns."

Mary frowned deeply. "Well, that's too close of a coincidence for comfort, isn't it?"

Dahlia nodded.

"But…the salesman. Deputy Hart and Hawk interviewed him. He had an alibi," Mary said. "Airtight. Deputy Hart told me so himself."

Anna nodded, because she'd heard the same from Hawk.

"People lie, though, right?" Dahlia offered.

"That they do," Mary said darkly. "I'm sure Hawk and Deputy Hart will look into it, a possible connection. Dig deeper. This is a good lead. The first good lead we've had." She smiled reassuringly at Anna, but Anna didn't feel reassured, God knew why.

Anna turned back to the computers, determined to figure out the glitch. Determined to *do* something instead of sit here and worry.

But only a few minutes later, they heard the low voices of the men returning. They sounded urgent, and when Jack opened the door and immediately met her gaze, she knew something was…terrible.

"No fire, but we've got a different situation." She swallowed at the bleakness in Jack's dark eyes. "I'm sorry. We can't find Hawk. He's not answering his phone. It looks like…"

"It looks like what?" she said, not sure if it came out as a whisper or a shriek. Because her heart was pounding in her ears.

"There was some blood. Some marks in the snow that made it look like he'd been…" Jack cleared his throat. "Dragged away."

"Then what are you all doing here?" Anna demanded, though she was glad Mary was standing there, holding her up. Because she felt like she might collapse. "We need to find him. We need to—"

"I've called some deputies in. And notified Hart. Palmer is getting a few horses saddled, and Grant and him are going to follow the tracks."

"You will saddle up a horse for me. I don't want to hear one damn argument," Anna said, forcing herself forward on shaky legs.

But Jack stopped her easily, his hand wrapped around her shoulder gently. "You aren't going, Anna. He wouldn't want you to."

She knew that was true. She *hated* that it was true, and that she really wasn't feeling up to getting on a horse, and probably shouldn't. She hated being held back like this. She needed to…

She looked up at her big brother. She knew he would do anything for her, but he wouldn't let her risk herself under the circumstances. She also knew that because she cared about Hawk, so would Jack.

So she had to trust Jack to take this on, since she couldn't. But that didn't mean she had to just give up and step aside and become the weeping pregnant lady in the corner.

"If I'm not going, *I'm* calling the shots. Palmer stays and helps me with the computer stuff. Maybe we can get something to go off there. Jack, you go with Grant to track Hawk. Your deputies don't need you micromanaging, so Mary will manage them once they get there. Cash can take Louisa and use the dogs to track or whatever he thinks is best. Understood?"

Jack looked at her for a very long time and she was afraid she'd just fall apart, start sobbing and never stop. Imagine every possible terrible outcome of this.

But Jack nodded. "All right, Annie. Understood." Then he cleared his throat. "Just a small…catch to that plan."

"What?"

"Cash is busy right now. He's patching up Pita. The dog's fine, just got a bit of a…gash."

Anna's knees went weak, but Mary and Dahlia held her up until she was steady again. Then she was pushing her way out of the room.

She heard people saying her name, Jack was still holding on to her arm, but she just kept fighting him off. She pushed her way out the back door and saw Cash kneeling next to poor little Pita. He had one of his dog first-aid kits open and was working on Pita while Louisa held a flashlight.

Anna stopped because she didn't want to interrupt what Cash was doing when he looked so intense and Pita was so *still*.

After a few minutes of everyone standing motionless and very quiet, Cash stood. "I stitched him up. He'll be okay." Cash smiled encouragingly up at her. "He will be okay. He just needs some rest."

"Who would hurt a little puppy?" She swallowed, because the answer was terrible no matter what, but whoever it was also had Hawk. A *bleeding* Hawk.

Palmer arrived with the horses, and though they weren't here yet, Anna could hear the sirens of Sunrise PD in the distance. Jack gave out orders—*her* orders, and in a sea of terror and horrible feelings, that was something.

Before Cash and Louisa went to get the search dogs, he reached over to Mary, who was now the one cradling Pita.

"You and Dahlia watch after Izzy?"

"You know we will."

Anna stood in the midst of her family coming together to solve this horrible problem, and she hated that she couldn't wade in there. But Palmer scooped up Pita from Mary, and then took Anna's arm with his free hand.

"Come on. Let's see what we can do with those computers."

And there was nothing else to do but that.

Chapter Thirteen

Hawk came to in a...barn? He opened his eyes and immediately closed them when the world swam. No matter where he was, it sure smelled like horse excrement. And his head ached like...well, like he'd been knocked in the back of the skull with something damn hard.

He worked to even his breathing, to center himself somewhere outside of the radiating pain. He had to stay conscious. He had to get his way out of this. Get back to Anna and make sure Pita was okay.

Had to make sure whoever had hurt Anna and Pita paid. A million times over.

When he opened his eyes for the second time, he was braced for the dizziness. The wave of nausea. The barn was dark, but he could make out shadows. If it was still dark, maybe he hadn't been unconscious for that long. Maybe he was in a barn on the Hudson property.

But when he moved his head a little bit, slowly and carefully to brace himself against the pain and dizziness, he could see the hint of light outside the cracks in the wood around him. Not quite morning, but the hint of new daylight.

Already? That would mean he'd spent far too much time unconscious.

Worse, so much worse than how much time had passed was the realization his hands were tied behind his back and fastened to something. He pulled at the bonds, testing them, but it was plastic or something of the like. Zip ties probably.

It wouldn't make it impossible to get out of here, but it was going to be a process.

"Awake, huh?" He realized now part of the light was the beam of a flashlight around a corner, or something. It bobbed and he realized he was in a kind of stall. So there were walls around him, except for the open door area in front of him.

Hawk squinted in the direction of the voice—female, high-pitched and wholly unbothered at the situation. A bright light flipped on above him and Hawk had to close his eyes against the blast of pain at the shocking change.

When he managed to blink his eyes back open, he assumed the woman standing in front of him was the owner of the voice. He studied her with some confusion. She definitely didn't look strong enough to cart his body around. She was on the shorter side, practically skin and bones with it. She had frizzy auburn hair and wasn't quite dressed for the cold with a long-sleeved T-shirt and some jeans.

But she was also very clearly high, so maybe that explained some things. *Some* things. Not the fact that she looked vaguely familiar. Something about the eyes. Where had he seen those eyes before?

He wanted to demand answers to a hundred questions, but he was with it enough to hold back. To consider. He needed to be smart about this. He wasn't *dead*. So that was something.

If he could get out of these ties, he could easily over-power this woman and escape. She wasn't possibly work-ing alone, but she *was* currently alone. Which meant time was of the essence.

"So, what do you want with me?" he asked, because it was the most direct question that all his other questions stemmed from. If this was about Anna, he wasn't sure how he was being dragged into it. Other than spending some time with her. Or maybe investigating?

The woman looked at her nails as if considering. "Oh, we want lots of things."

We, he noted.

"But we want different things. I'm interested in your bank account." She dropped her hand and studied him. "How much are you willing to pay to get out of this situ-ation?"

"I'm not big on paying off two-bit criminals with drug addictions," he returned, equally as casual as she was being.

Her eyes narrowed, a familiar blue. Why was this woman familiar?

But Hawk figured it was best to keep poking until she exploded. She wasn't strong enough to do any real dam-age unless she brandished a weapon, and he couldn't see where she'd be hiding one on her.

"I know this isn't really about me," he said.

"If you'd been smart, it *wouldn't* be about you. Never should have gotten involved with Anna Hudson. Or *any* Hudson. A bunch of stuck-up, do-gooder *liars*. It doesn't matter what you do—you're always an outsider there. They never, ever give you a real chance."

Then it dawned on him. He'd seen those eyes in a little girl, who'd sighed dreamily at him over dinner. And he'd not that long ago discussed the possibility of this woman's involvement. "Chessa."

Her eyebrows rose. "How'd you know that?" she asked with more curiosity than malice.

He smiled, because if she was really just interested in money, why not pretend to be friendly? "I know lots of things."

"All right, pretty boy." She flashed a grin. "Don't think you're flirting your way out of this one."

He tried very hard not to pull a face, but it was difficult considering how little *flirting his way out of this one* factored into his plan.

Which was currently rip his bonds off whatever they were tied to and run like hell before whoever Chessa was working for got here.

"So, how much would it take to let me go?" he asked, because that seemed the simplest route to getting what he wanted.

She studied him, frowning. "You just said you don't pay off criminals."

"But you're not a criminal, are you? I checked you out. A few brushes with the law, sure, but you've never done any time for it."

Her chin came up. "Right? Tell that to my uptight ex-husband. I could take care of that brat of ours if I wanted to. But I got to make a living, and don't I deserve to have a little fun after being shackled to that place like some kind of servant?"

Hawk tried to keep his expression bland, but it was hard not to react to the way she spoke of sweet little Izzy. "You're lucky you got out when you did," he managed without sounding angry.

She snorted. "Would be if he'd give me what I was owed. I would have gotten it too if your little girlfriend hadn't gotten in my way. Do you know what kind of money I could get for a cute little girl like…?" She trailed off, blinked, as if realizing she'd said too much. Maybe because Hawk couldn't keep his expression cool or calm.

She was talking about *selling* her child. That wasn't just a bad mother; it was disgusting and inhuman. Hawk didn't speak. He knew it would come out venom. So he breathed, and he tried to dissociate. Tried to approach this like a case.

Not people he'd come to care about.

But it was impossible. He just kept hearing Izzy asking him if he played the drums. Picturing Anna crying in her sleep. Those family dinners that were so overwhelming he wanted to run screaming in the opposite direction… and yet looked forward to. Every night.

"So, what's the plan here?" he asked, working to keep his voice even instead of a vicious growl. "With me?"

Chessa studied him, then shrugged. "I'm not privy to all the plans. Not a criminal, remember? All he cares about is making your baby mama pay."

Over my dead body. "If you get me out of here, we can go straight to the closest ATM. I'll give you everything I've got." He wasn't even lying about it. He didn't care about money. He cared about keeping Anna and Izzy safe.

She scowled, crossed her arms over her chest. "I don't trust you."

"I don't trust you either, but I'll pay."

She considered it. Then without a word she turned on a heel and disappeared behind the corner.

While she was gone, Hawk jerked at the ties around his

wrists. He couldn't tell what he was tied to, but he kept pulling in the futile hope that he could break *something*. He didn't even need his hands free. He just needed to be able to run.

Chessa reappeared with a gun in her hand. She didn't point it at him, but he didn't like the idea of her with a gun. She was too unpredictable, and she'd be coming down off that high soon enough.

"I'll take you to the ATM, but any funny business and I shoot you. He finds me, he's going to kill me. So I need the money and time to get the hell out of here. You don't help me get it, you're dead."

"Why don't you tell me who this 'he' is so I can protect you?"

She laughed. "You think I know? All I know is some guy comes up to me at the bar and propositions me. Not in the usual way. Asks if I hate the Hudsons as much as he does. Boy, do I."

She inched closer, the weapon shaking in her hand making Hawk a lot more nervous than he'd like to be. He knew he could take this woman once he was out of the bonds, but the chances of her *accidentally* killing him before he got the opportunity felt a little too probable.

"Who's 'he'?" Hawk asked, watching the gun in her hand even as she pulled out a knife with the other.

"He says to just call him Boss and do what he says. *I* can follow directions and orders, because I'm not holier than thou like all those people you've been hanging around with. You pay me, I'll do whatever."

She crouched next to him, gun pointed right at his chest. She reached around, began to cut his bonds.

"So, he has something against all of them? Or just

Anna?" he asked, working hard to stay calm. To not tele-graph his intentions, or to worry about the possibility of a bullet going right through his heart.

Chessa shrugged. The plastic snapped and Hawk's hands fell to the ground. She pointed the gun right at his forehead, and hell, he did not like that.

"Get to your feet."

He followed orders. She took a good five steps away, clearly afraid he'd overpower her. And he would, whether she was five steps or five yards. But he wanted a little more information first.

"I'm not sure if he hates all the Hudsons or just knew I did. He's got a bee in his bonnet over Anna, that's for sure."

"Why?"

Chessa rolled her eyes, pocketing the knife. Her hand was shaking harder now, and she was sweating. The gun was still precariously pointed at his face.

She jerked her head toward the corner she'd appeared from. "Walk that way. I'm behind you. One false move, and a bullet goes into your brain. We gotta act fast. Like I said, I'm dead if he finds me before I can run."

Hawk knew he shouldn't ask. It was like tempting fate, but… "Why take the chance?" he asked as he moved for-ward like she'd told him to.

"His plan is taking too long, and he won't tell me when I'll get my payout. I need money like yesterday."

Translation: she'd run out of ways to get high and cared more about that than anything else.

Hawk would use it. He glanced over his shoulder. She was holding the gun with both hands now.

"I thought this was about revenge on the Hudsons," he said, stepping out of the barn and into the even colder night. There was the hint of daylight on the horizon, but not full morning yet.

"For him, maybe. And sure, I wouldn't have minded seeing Anna taken down a few pegs, but I'd rather take my money and run. They'll have security too tight right now anyway. No chance of getting Izzy. I'll come back for her some other time."

Like hell you will.

"It's too dark to see," he said. Hawk pretended to stumble a little, like he was too dizzy to stay upright. A little to the right, a little to the left.

"Stop that!" she yelled at him.

"I think I'm going to be sick."

"I think I'm going to shoot you and just be done—"

But he was too fast in the dark, too big, and she was too messed up to really have any clue what she was doing. He might have even felt sorry for her, if she hadn't talked about her daughter with such cold, disgusting plans.

He had the gun out of her hands in less than a minute. When she launched herself at him, he easily side-stepped. She tumbled into the snowy ground without any help from him.

He knelt on her back, making quick work of pulling the knife from her and searching her for any other weapons or anything he could use. He got a flashlight, which would be a help.

But nothing he could use to tie her up with. She was kicking and screaming, but he barely registered any of it, so intent on his plan.

He dragged her back to the barn by the legs, even as she tried to kick them out of his grasp. She wasn't strong enough.

She bucked and tried to roll, but he got her back in the barn. He looked around for something, anything, to hold her, but it was mostly empty. He found a little bit of frayed rope. Not long enough to tie her to anything, but he could maybe tie the door closed.

He let go of her legs, but she just kept thrashing around on the ground. Waste of energy. "I hope your boss is as useless as you are," he said.

She spit at him, but he'd expected that and managed to jump out of the way. None of this would hold her for long, but he'd be long gone by then, and she might be careless, and addled by her drug addiction, but hopefully she knew well enough not to come tearing after him in the cold winter night.

He pulled the barn door closed behind him. He flipped the flashlight on, shoved it in his mouth to hold it as he worked to get the rope through the handle and the small, rusted hook. It was barely long enough to make one little knot, but it might hold for a bit.

She jerked the door, and the rope held. Hawk dropped the flashlight from his mouth to his hand.

"You will *never* get your hands on Izzy," he called through the door. "I will personally make sure of it for the rest of my damn life."

"They're going to chew you up and spit you out," she screamed, rattling the door. "That's what they do."

He didn't bother to respond. He swung the flashlight around his surroundings.

He had to figure out where the hell he was so he could get back to Anna before the "boss" did. He didn't have a sense of where he was at all. The chance of him picking the wrong direction and getting lost on top of everything else was a little too high.

But Chessa was beating on the door, screaming. He had to put some distance between him and her.

Someone had brought him here—and not just her. So there had to be prints in the snow somewhere. He was no expert at tracking, but it would give him an idea of the right direction. Hopefully.

He walked around the barn, found some tire tracks. Only one set of prints, though. Had she really handled this herself? He shook his head. It didn't matter. It only mattered that he got back to Anna.

He began to follow the tire tracks. Even if it didn't lead him back to the Hudson Ranch, it would lead him to a road, surely.

As long as he didn't freeze to death first, he supposed.

He wasn't sure how long he walked. His head pounded, and he was getting weaker the more he trudged through the hard-packed snow.

The first yip he heard he figured was a coyote or a figment of his imagination. Delirium even. The second yip came with the appearance of a dog.

One of Cash's dogs. Hawk nearly fell to his knees. "Hiya, boy. I don't know your name, but I am sure as hell glad to see you."

A horse appeared through the trees, Louisa the rider. She let out a sharp whistle, then swung off the horse. "Well, you gave us quite a scare," she said. Her voice was easy and calm. She surveyed her surroundings with assessing eyes and didn't let on that she was worried.

"Had me tied up in a barn." He swallowed, afraid he

was about to lose his dinner. "Managed to get away. Just one person for now, but there's a boss somewhere."

"You're a resourceful fellow." She came up to him, and even though he was desperately trying to maintain an air of strength, Louisa must have sensed he wasn't up for the fight. She slid her arm around his waist, urging him to lean on her. "Guess you need a ride back, huh?"

Hawk had never felt his knees go weak before, but they just about gave out on him. "Yeah…yeah, I do."

Chapter Fourteen

Anna wanted to take a baseball bat to every last computer and monitor in this worthless security room.

Palmer sighed next to her. "Why don't you take a break, huh? You're running ragged."

"A break? A break? Hawk is out there somewhere and I…" God, when had she become such a crybaby? "He was bleeding." She covered her face in her hands because she just couldn't take this.

What if he died? What if he was already dead? And it would be all because of her. And he wouldn't get to be a father, and he wouldn't get…

"Anna." Palmer squeezed her shoulder, hard enough to get through the haze of terror. "I know how you feel. Better than most."

She knew that was true, even if she wanted to feel like she was the only one in the whole world who understood this horrible, terrible fear.

But Louisa had been taken, too. Not that long ago. Palmer had suffered through this terrible, debilitating fear, and in the end, she'd been okay. Louisa had been okay.

Of course, that had been about Louisa's family, and though Palmer had been terrified and worried about Louisa, just like

Anna had, it wasn't like Louisa had been kidnapped because of *him*. Palmer hadn't felt *guilt* on top of everything else.

It was just taking too long, and so many people she loved were out there in harm's way because…somehow she'd done something so wrong along the way, now everyone was paying for her mistakes.

She sucked in a breath. Okay, she was in a panic spiral. It was dumb to blame herself, she knew, but if she was doing that, she wasn't thinking about Hawk dead, so that was nice.

He couldn't be dead. He couldn't… She pushed away from the computer. She needed to move. This felt all too much like childhood all over again. Being told to wait, to wonder, not to have any say in what went on around her.

All because she was pregnant? All because she was perfectly happy risking her life, but not her baby's. *Hawk's baby*. Their baby. And there was no place to put this fear, this fury. It just churned inside her like acid.

The chime of Palmer's phone made her jump. She whirled to him as he pulled it out, read the text. "They found him," Palmer said, looking up at her and giving her a reassuring smile. "They're bringing him back. No other details. But he's okay and they're bringing him back. So just take a breath, huh?"

She tried, but all the breath had clogged in her lungs. She wanted to feel relief, but there was a frozen band of fear holding her hostage. Until she saw him…

"Come on," Palmer said, taking her arm and pulling her out of the security room and into the dining room. Izzy sat in the corner of the room gently petting Pita, while Mary set up a coffee station.

"Sit down," Mary ordered, and Anna had no doubt she was talking to her, not Palmer. "You should be sleeping."

"How could I possibly sleep?" Anna muttered.

"She'll settle once she sees him," Palmer said reassuringly to Mary.

Mary didn't have anything to say to that as she fussed with an array of sweeteners. Her way of dealing with her nerves. Anna wished she had any kind of constructive way to deal with the feelings battering her.

"How's Pita doing?" Anna asked.

Izzy smiled up at her. "Still groggy but doing much better. Poor guy." She cuddled him to her chest, gently. "How could anyone hurt him, Aunt Anna?"

"I don't know, honey." She was in no space to have positive thoughts about humans as a species when so many seemed bent on hurting good people, innocent animals.

But Hawk was okay. No one would text that to Palmer if it wasn't true. But what if he was seriously hurt? What if—

The door opened. Hawk entered first, but even as she was halfway across the room to him, she could see Louisa was kind of keeping him upright. He was pale—way too pale, but he was on his own two feet. Here. Alive. Pita let out a sharp bark, skittering toward his owner, but Anna got there first. She wrapped her arms around Hawk and cried. She'd be embarrassed about how much and how loudly later. She clung to him like some kind of lunatic, but she didn't care. He was here.

And he held her right back. "I'm all right. I'm all right. Take a breath, Blondie."

But that only made her cry even more. Especially since she could tell he was barely capable of standing, and there was a trail of blood down the back of his jacket. "You need a doctor. You need…"

"We'll get it all taken care of," Louisa said, gently pulling Anna off Hawk. "Jack's grabbing an EMT. Won't be more than a minute or two."

Anna swallowed, trying to get a hold of herself while Palmer and Cash nudged Hawk into a chair. Izzy came over and picked Pita up and deposited the puppy on Hawk's lap.

Hawk smiled at her. "Thanks," he said. "He okay?"

"I stitched him up," Cash said. "Had a little gash, but he'll heal quick. I don't know what kind of sick, twisted person would hurt a puppy."

Anna noted the odd way Hawk looked at Cash, then Izzy, but she didn't know what it meant. Then a parade of people came in. Jack and Grant, followed by a cop and an EMT. The EMT crossed to Hawk, nudging her farther back.

"So what happened?" Jack demanded as the EMT began to check him out. Anna moved to the other side of him so she could hold his hand. She just…had to hold on to him.

"Maybe we could discuss this later," Hawk said through gritted teeth, clearly in pain.

"But—"

Hawk looked at her, those dark blue eyes pleading, when she couldn't have ever imagined Hawk Steele being pleading. "Not here. Not now." He looked to Jack. "Okay?" Then his gaze turned to Izzy, giving the girl an odd look she couldn't read, and suddenly…

She had the horrible suspicion she understood.

"Cash," Anna managed, though her voice was strangled. "Maybe Izzy should take Pita somewhere with less excitement."

Hawk watched Cash's expression carefully. He didn't think the man knew. *Hoped* he just thought Anna was trying to keep Izzy from getting too involved in a grisly story that didn't involve her.

Izzy crossed over to him and held her hands out for Pita. Hawk wanted to keep the puppy in his lap. Just feel his ribs rise and fall and know that he was okay, but he couldn't say anything he had to say in front of Izzy. Wasn't sure he really wanted to say it in front of Cash either.

Clearly Anna had caught on to his meaning.

He shifted Pita back into Izzy's arms. He managed to smile at the girl, even though the EMT washing out his wound hurt like hell. "Thanks for taking good care of him, Izzy."

She beamed at him, then went with Cash out of the room.

Hawk waited. Let the EMT work. Let silence settle over. He watched Anna, tearstained, watch her brother and niece exit. No doubt making sure they were out of earshot before they discussed anything.

She'd sobbed all over him like he'd come back from the dead. Held on to him so tight he'd nearly passed out from the pain of it. But he hadn't told her she was hurting him because...

She cared about him. A woman like Anna Hudson didn't fall apart over some guy who accidentally knocked her up. Not like that. She was too strong, too bullheaded and determined to appear tough. Crying like that... She cared about him.

Maybe she didn't love him, but it felt like the *possibility* was there. And he... It was just another one of those life lessons. He hadn't wanted love or security—stopped believing in those things after his mother had died.

Then Anna had blown into his life and knocked everything on its axis, and he could only be grateful, because she was everything. And that heart he'd been so sure he'd frozen out throbbed painfully in his chest.

Maybe she didn't love him yet, but she could. Because he sure as hell loved her.

"This might hurt a little," the EMT said.

It did, but so did the dull pain he'd been dealing with since he'd gained consciousness.

"Concussion, no doubt. I'd recommend a trip to the hospital, have some tests run. That's a hell of a bump."

"No," Hawk said.

"Hawk," Anna began, no doubt ready to swoop in and play protector. "You—"

"No. I'm not going to the hospital. I'm fine."

"Don't be stubborn," Anna said, frowning at him. But she never let go of his hand, like she couldn't stand the thought of losing that connection.

God knew he couldn't.

"Rich coming from you, Blondie. Look, when this is all over? I'll see whatever doctors you want, but there is too much danger and too many questions still to answer." He turned to find Jack in the room. "I'll start at the beginning. You want to take notes or do you want to get one of your deputies?"

"I'll take the notes," Jack returned. "I'll record it too," he said, pulling his phone out of his uniform pocket. "It'll hold up in court."

Hawk was glad Jack was thinking that far down the line. He couldn't seem to think clearly. Not fully. But he could relate exactly what had happened, and then maybe once his head stopped feeling like it'd been split in two, he'd be able to make sense of it all.

"I wish I had found some answers in all this, but I think I've only found more questions. And more complications. More danger." He blew out a breath. "I was outside, circling the house with Pita like we discussed. Pita growled and I heard something, so I went to investigate, and I told Pita to stay back. Damn dog listened to me, too."

Hawk took a ragged breath because Pita was alive and okay. Anna was here. As long as they were safe, little else mattered. "I heard two different sounds—one in the trees, one closer to Pita. The dog yelped and I knew it was someone hurting Pita. I turned toward the dog, and that was my mistake, what they were likely going for, because something hit me from behind. Hard. When I came to, I was in a barn. How did you guys find me?"

"Followed your…" Louisa trailed off and looked at Anna as if she was reconsidering her words. "Tracks," she finished.

He figured she'd meant to say "blood" but hadn't wanted Anna to get more upset. Hawk nodded, pausing to take a sip of water because he was afraid if he didn't he'd lose the battle with nausea.

"First it was footprints. Then it was tire tracks," Louisa added, for the sake of Jack's recording. "We took the horses to follow those tracks. We found him just west of the property."

"My deputies are treating the barn like a crime scene. It isn't our property, but it is close," Jack said. "What happened in the barn?"

"When I woke up, there was a woman. Short, skinny. No way she acted alone."

He looked away from Jack and toward Anna. She was struggling with this, clearly, but when she spoke it was clear.

"It was Chessa," Anna said flatly.

All the Hudsons in the room had a different negative reaction to that, but Hawk could only watch Anna. He hated that this hurt her even deeper than it already had.

"She's working for someone," Hawk continued to explain. "I'm not sure she cared so much about what they were doing. She just wanted a payout. Clearly she's got a drug problem. I offered her money, and she untied me. Which was how I got away." He turned to look at Jack again. "I gave one of your deputies her description. She's back in that barn."

Jack nodded. "They've got her. She's in the process of being arrested. They'll take her down to the station and we'll question her there."

Hawk moved to stand, had to fight off the dizziness. "I want to be a part of—"

Palmer's hand curled on his shoulder, gently pushed him back down into a sitting position.

"Sorry, pal. You're on bed rest until further notice."

"You can't just—"

"We can. We will. We do," Anna said. "In fact, you should be in bed right now. You've explained what happened. Now you'll rest."

"Anna, you aren't in charge of me."

"Maybe not, but consider yourself outnumbered." She pointed at Jack, Mary, Palmer and Louisa. "No one gives one little care who you think is in charge. You're not going anywhere except bed. If we all have to carry you up to bed and lock you in."

"Doesn't sound very recuperative," Hawk muttered. But he also didn't know how to argue with the wall of Hudson disapproval. Or how to deal with the strange wave of warmth that swept through him, leaving him feeling even weaker than he had.

"Hart is meeting me down at the station," Jack said. "We'll fill you in on the details for your investigation once you've rested a bit. Hart can handle communicating your injuries with your boss at the county."

"We've got to figure out who she's working for, and fast. Chessa was very clear that her boss is a he, and that his only goal was to hurt Anna *and* any of you. We *have* to find him."

"We will."

"Come on," Palmer said, and suddenly he was being lifted on one side by Palmer, Anna sliding onto the other side.

"I can walk," Hawk muttered.

But no one listened. Mary said she'd bring up some water and cold compresses. Palmer and Anna just kept moving him out of the kitchen and up the stairs.

No one had taken care of him for a very, very long time, and suddenly he had this…pseudo family.

He didn't know what to do with it, except let himself be led around the Hudson house like he had no will of his own.

"He's filthy. He needs a bath," Anna said once they reached the top of the stairs.

"Count me out on that one."

Anna rolled her eyes. "Go grab him some clothes. He's got everything in that ugly duffel bag in my room."

She led Hawk into the bathroom and drew him a bath—which was possibly the weirdest damn moment of his life. But the warm water felt nice, and she kept the lights off so the room was dark.

"No falling asleep," she said. Then she took a washcloth and some soap and started cleaning him up.

"This is weird," he muttered. Because she was giving him a bath, and not in a sexy way he might have preferred if his head didn't currently feel like it had been used as a piñata.

"Well, don't go getting bashed in the head and things won't be weird."

"Hey, you got bashed in the head first. I don't remember giving *you* a bath."

"I'm glad it's a contest," she replied, all prim disgust. "And since it is, I win, because I ended up in the hospital. Where *you* should be."

He heard the worry in her tone, wished he could find a way around it. "I really am fine."

She scoffed. "Hardly."

Hawk closed his eyes, but he couldn't stop himself from making sure… "Pita really okay?"

"Cash isn't a practicing vet, but he has all the training. If he says Pita will be fine, Pita will be fine. If he was worried, he would have taken him to the animal hospital in Hardy."

He sighed, the mention of Cash twisting his gut into knots all over again. "I'm sorry."

"For what?"

"That it was Chessa. They'll have to know. She's…"

Hawk swallowed. "She said some awful things, Anna. She doesn't care about Izzy at all." Worse even than his own father's not caring. The way she'd talked about that innocent little girl, her *own* innocent little girl.

"We know it. But they've got Chessa locked up for the time being. So Izzy is safe, and we'll always keep her safe. We always have. It's what we do."

He opened his eyes and looked at her in the dim room as she carefully washed him without getting close to the stitches in the back of his head. "You've got a hell of a family, Blondie."

She lifted her gaze and held his for a long silent moment before she eventually spoke. "I know it. And now you've got them, too."

Chapter Fifteen

She got him dried off and dressed. He didn't even make a joke about being naked, which had her nerves humming. Was he really okay? Should she *make* him go to the hospital?

But she helped him into her bed and arranged everything. She kept the room dark. Rest was the only thing for a concussion. So she crawled into bed with him, even as the sun was starting to shine into her window.

"Tell me if I'm hurting you," she said, resting her head on his shoulder. His arm came around and pulled her closer.

"You?" he said, pressing a kiss to her forehead. "Never."

She wasn't sure how long they lay there. She hoped he was sleeping, but she didn't think he was. There was still a tenseness about him, even if his breathing was even.

Anna knew no matter how tired she was, she wouldn't sleep until he did. Maybe even then she wouldn't, because she wanted to know what Chessa was saying down at the station. She wanted to know if anyone had told Cash yet.

She wanted a million things, but at the end of the day, she wouldn't leave Hawk. He needed rest, and she had to know he was getting it.

"You know, I realized something downstairs," he said, an oddly thoughtful tone to his voice.

She expected him to deliver a joke, or ask about Pita, or something rather bland. Maybe something vague about the investigation. A possible lead.

"I love you."

So instead, she was rendered absolutely speechless. She'd just started to come around to *care* and he was upgrading things to *love*.

"That's a first for me," he continued, just lying there, saying these things. Like it was normal. Like she'd know what to do with it. "Just FYI. Can't promise I'm any good at it."

That cut through a little of her panic. Her heart ached, for a million different reasons even she couldn't untangle. She pressed her palm to his stubbled cheek. "You're very good at it," she said through the lump in her throat. "Hawk, I…" But she didn't know how to *say* things like that. She didn't know how to circumvent the panic coursing through her.

Love. *Love.* She knew all about love. What little she could remember about her parents was love, and her siblings had always been the core of everything loving and good. But how did you *choose* that horrible worry and ache that went along with loving someone and losing someone? How did anyone stand it?

Or did you even have a choice?

"Hawk," she repeated, because she knew she had to say something. Explain in some way that wasn't actually… saying those three substantial and terrifying words.

Even if they were true.

"Don't insult me, Anna. And don't lie to spare my feelings. It isn't you."

She sat up and stared down at him. He was scowling, but his eyes were closed. *Insult* him? *Lie* to him? Of all the…

"You have no idea what I'm trying to say."

"I know what you're trying *not* to say," he returned in that obnoxious law enforcement voice like he was so much smarter than her. Detached and in control of everything.

When no one was in control. Life was a series of... dangerous events and horrible people and fear and worry and...and... He was lying there *concussed*, acting like he had it all figured out.

"BS! You don't know..." She had to get out of bed because she wanted to explode, and there was no staving it off, but she wasn't going to hurt him while she did it. "*You* don't know how to love someone? I have been fighting the world since I was eight years old. And I've had this very enviable cushion in my family, but everything I've done is because losing hurts so much and I want to be the one to control the hurt. I have *never* been so damn afraid as I was tonight. All I could think was you'd be dead, and I wouldn't even have a chance to marry you."

He opened one eye. "So you're going to marry me?"

She stared at him for a full shocked minute. The nerve. "You're *impossible*."

"Yeah, but so are you. Maybe we were made for each other."

She didn't know how he did it, but the anger just leaked out of her. Maybe it was the fact that he looked terrible, or that he was in her bed, or that...he'd said he loved her and then listened to her whole explosion and hadn't exploded himself.

Maybe they *were* made for each other. She wasn't sure she was ready to believe that for certain, but she liked the idea of it, anyway.

She sat back on the bed. She didn't cuddle up to him,

but knelt next to him, looking down at him until he opened both eyes.

"I love you," she said, and she'd always considered herself brave, but she was sure uttering those three things was the bravest thing she'd ever done. "But we have a lot to talk about first, before we agree to any...marrying."

He closed his eyes again, on a careless shrug. "Well, that's progress, anyway."

He really was impossible.

"Lie down, Anna," he murmured. "Let's get some sleep."

She didn't appreciate being ordered around, but she saw a flash of how terrible he'd looked when he'd walked in that door. So she lay down. Curled up next to him.

His arms came around her. "Chessa was very clear. Whoever this man is, he wants to hurt you. You have to take that seriously."

She rested her palm on her stomach. "I do." Then she took his hand and laced it with hers and placed their entwined hands on her stomach.

And when he finally fell asleep, so did she.

HAWK WOKE UP a while later with a thundering headache that got worse as he opened his eyes and found the room flooded with light. Anna was no longer beside him, but Pita was curled up where Anna should be.

It eased his frustration a little. As if the puppy sensed him being awake, he wriggled closer and closer until he was curled up in the crook of Hawk's shoulder.

"You're a good dog," he murmured. "But you're never coming along on another investigation, I hope you know. Not until you're bigger and meaner, anyway." He couldn't let himself think about it—that little yelp of pain. How much worse everything could have been.

The bedroom door eased open and Anna stepped in, carrying a tray. "Oh, good. You're awake. Here's breakfast."

He sat up in bed, trying not to wince against the pain. He tried even harder to sound his authoritative self. "I need an update on what's going on with the investigation."

"And I need a mansion in Hawaii to winter in. Doesn't mean I'm getting it."

He scowled at her. "I am the arson investigator on this case, and I'm not going to be shoved out just because of a little head injury."

"Little?" she snorted, shaking her head. "Yours was worse than mine and *I* went to the hospital."

"I'm doing fine, as I'm not pregnant and didn't inhale a roomful of smoke."

She studied him with pursed lips. "You're doing better, but hardly fine." She put the tray on the bed next to him. "You need to eat, hydrate and keep resting."

There was no point arguing with her, or maybe arguing with her just hurt his head. Besides, sometimes it was better not to argue—and just do what needed doing. She couldn't babysit him all day. He'd find a way to get the information he wanted.

But maybe it wouldn't hurt to eat a little first. He started with the toast as Pita tried to climb up on the tray. Anna plucked him off the bed and cradled him in her arms. "You have to eat yours on the floor." She put him down on the ground, then took the bowl off the tray he realized was wet dog food and put it in front of Pita. Then she carefully settled herself on the bed without dislodging the tray.

He ate a little, drank some juice and formulated his plan. Even if he got a little out of her, she wouldn't tell him everything. But a little would give him something to go off of. "The way I see it, you have two choices. Give me an update, or I get one myself in whatever ways I feel necessary."

She laughed and gently ruffled his hair. Like he was a child. He scowled even harder at her.

"I think you underestimate the Hudson machine. You're our prisoner until you're better. Everyone is going to make sure you rest, so whatever you *feel* necessary ain't happening, bud."

"I think you underestimate me."

Anna considered, or maybe she pretended to consider. "You see that puppy right there? The one you didn't want. The one Mary steamrolled you into?"

He didn't bother to respond to that. So maybe he *had* been steamrolled into adopting a dog. And a few other things, but...

"There won't be any you getting your way until you get the all clear from the doctor."

Hawk considered this with the sinking feeling that... she was probably right. There were too many of them. He was outnumbered.

"It's called being taken care of, Hawk. And if you're sticking around, you're going to have to get used to it."

"From your whole family?"

"Yup. We come as a unit. If that scares you off, then that's on you."

"It doesn't scare me off," he muttered. Maybe he didn't *relish* the thought of her whole family "taking care," but he was hardly going to run away with his tail between his legs just because she had some overbearing siblings.

It would take a lot more than that to scare off Hawk Steele.

"Now, if you're a good boy and finish your breakfast, I'll give you an update."

Hawk stared at her and had the uncomfortable realization that if he hadn't been trying to force her to give him information, she probably would have offered that deal in the first place.

So he ate, though he wasn't happy about it. Once he was done, he raised an eyebrow at her and she sighed.

"All right. A deal is a deal. Jack says Chessa isn't talking. He said the running theory is she actually doesn't know anything. She was just a pawn, so we're not much closer than we were on that front."

Unfortunately, that was the impression he got from Chessa as well. "What's the other front?"

"Mary, Dahlia and I found a possible connection and Mary passed that on to Hart last night, so they're looking into it."

"Explain the connection."

She didn't say anything as she got up off the bed. She picked Pita up and put him back on the bed. Then she skirted the bed, came to the other side and leaned over him. She looked him right in the eye. "No."

He could have argued with her, but maybe on this he was finally learning a lesson. "I at least need my phone."

"No screens. You need rest, and that's it."

"I have to call my boss."

"According to Hart, he's informed all the necessary

parties that you're out on medical leave until a doctor says otherwise."

"Anna."

"Be a good patient." She leaned over, brushed a kiss over his forehead. "You and Pita." But before she could pull away, he reached for her wrists to keep her there. Maybe he couldn't get through to her about the investigation in this moment, and the investigation *was* the most important thing in this moment, but he wasn't a man who liked losing. He had to win a point somewhere.

"Was I dreaming, or did you agree to marry me last night?"

"You must have been dreaming." She tugged her hands, but he didn't let her go. "I very specifically said we had a lot of things to discuss first."

"First."

"Yes, and *first* comes before *second*, which still wouldn't be an agreement." She kept tugging, but he also knew she was afraid to use her full strength against him since he was injured, which gave him the opportunity to hold on to her and keep her there and face *this*—them—if nothing else.

"Okay, let's start with first. What's the first thing you want to talk about?"

She stopped tugging for a minute, looking at him like she couldn't decide exactly how to feel about any of this. He didn't mind.

She *had* said she loved him, and while he might have been frustrated with her initial hesitation, maybe even a little insecure about it, he'd watched her explode about... *fighting the world* and he'd understood a deeper facet of her.

So he didn't think she was lying, that love was something she'd ever feel comfortable lying about. And she definitely wasn't the kind of woman who convinced herself she was in love with a man to be nice, to be taken care of.

He imagined love was as much a surprise out of left field for her as it was for him.

"I want to live here. Not Bent. Not Sunrise. The ranch." She said it so seriously, like it was some kind of challenge.

"With me?"

She tugged again. He didn't let go.

"No, with Bigfoot, genius."

"That's easy. I don't care where I live." He thought about all her siblings and living permanently under the same roof and tried not to grimace. Maybe not *ideal*, but how could he argue with her wanting to stay here with her family, her roots?

Maybe if he had roots he'd want the same, but he only had himself. "Because I love you, Anna. I don't have ties to my house, to Bent, to anyone. So you want to live here, it means something to you, that's more than all the stuff that doesn't mean anything to me." And their child would grow up a part of all this?

It was no sacrifice. It was a gift.

She frowned at him. "You know, the plan was to make sure you realized I was a bad bet, and you wouldn't *want* to marry me."

It amused him that she'd had a plan. Even if it had been a terrible one. Who wouldn't fall for her? "Major fail, huh?"

"Yeah, major." She heaved out a sigh. "All right, if I tell you about this possible connection in the case, you have to *promise*. No screens for at least twenty-four more hours. You stick to bed. You eat, you rest. You be a good patient."

He held up his hand. "Scout's honor."

"You were never a Boy Scout," she said, eyes narrowed in suspicion.

"On the contrary, I was. For one whole year. Before I got kicked out of my pack for starting a few unauthorized fires at camp, just to see what would melt. And what wouldn't. What can I say? I've always been interested in fire."

She let out a delighted laugh, then settled in next to him. And told him all about the case, curled up with him.

Where she belonged.

Chapter Sixteen

The days passed with no break in the case. Anna was almost relieved, if only because it gave Hawk a chance to recover. As much as she wanted answers, needed to know the people who'd hurt them, in those first few days all she could bring herself to care about was Hawk getting better.

After her harassing, and his boss's insistence, he'd finally gone and gotten checked out by a real doctor. A few days later, he had a clean bill of health to go back to work, and he'd spent the entire day away from the ranch, working.

Anna was shocked and appalled to find herself missing him. What kind of lovesick teenager was she becoming? The closer it got to dinnertime, the less she could concentrate on any task. What if he had some kind of relapse? What if he was hurt? What if...?

What if you got a hold of yourself? she demanded internally.

"Why don't you go set the table?" Mary said pleasantly. The kind of pleasant that was an order, not a request. The kind of pleasant lesser men did not see through.

Anna looked down at the cucumber she was supposed to be slicing and realized she'd chopped it to bits. It wasn't her turn to set the table. Mary just wanted her out from underfoot so she'd stop ruining dinner preparations.

"Yeah, why don't I?" she muttered, then started gathering everything they'd need. She set out plates and glasses, then the silverware, all the way chastising herself.

If she was going to do this whole till-death-do-they-part thing with Hawk, *God*, she had to figure out a way to deal with his job. And he'd have to find a way to deal with hers. They would have to be apart sometimes. They would have to deal with their worry more constructively than she was doing today.

She couldn't feel this way all the time. She'd burst.

But actually witnessing him be injured was like opening up a floodgate of anxiety and worry. How did people do this love thing? It was excruciating.

She heard someone enter the dining room, but focused on her work, focused on harnessing all these terrible new feelings she didn't know what to do with. She didn't want to deal with small talk with one of her siblings or anyone who lived here.

"Hey."

She practically dropped the entire collection of flatware at the sound of Hawk's voice. She had to squeeze on to it to keep from rushing over to him. What was wrong with her? Slowly, she put the forks and knives down and turned to face him, forcing herself to smile casually. "Hi, honey. How was your day?"

He smirked. There was almost an entire room between them and they stood frozen, just staring at each other, all this space between them. Her heart fluttered in her chest. He was honestly the most attractive man she'd ever laid eyes on. And she loved him.

Loved.

"Annoying," he said. "Hart's as frustrated as we are. The

CS Computer Systems is the only real lead, real connection, but everyone's clean. At least as far as we can find. If there's something there, we haven't found it yet."

Anna nodded. That *was* frustrating. Somehow, they had to find a break in this case. So she could go back to having a normal life not worried someone was out to get her. Not wrapped up so much in this man she couldn't *concentrate*.

"And you weren't there," he said, his voice quiet but firm, his blue eyes intense even with the big table between them.

She let out the breath that had gotten clogged in her lungs, all anxiety and stress and *want*. "You weren't here."

She figured they both moved then, since they met somewhere in the middle, but it wasn't a conscious choice. It was like moon to tide, a magnet. His arms banded around her, and she pushed to her toes and pressed her mouth to his.

It hadn't even been twelve hours since she'd seen him, but it felt like centuries, and she just…needed him. Needed this. And it was scary and wonderful all at the same time. To need someone like this. To love someone like this.

To have something like this.

It was like she hadn't seen him in decades, and she didn't know what that was. Just that it *was*. And she didn't want him to stop touching her, kissing her—

"Do you mind?"

She managed to pull her mouth away from Hawk's, look over his shoulder at her brother. Grant's face was all pinched, and he was looking at the ceiling in an embarrassed kind of horror. Poor Grant, who loved his girlfriend, clearly, but *still* didn't engage in much PDA. At least around them.

"Yeah, I do mind," Anna returned. "Why don't you scram?"

Grant scowled at her, and she thought she might have been able to get rid of him, but then Jack entered. His bland expression turned into a scowl.

"You have a *room*," he pointed out.

"What's the fun in a room?" she returned, but Hawk was disentangling himself, setting her away from him. *Coward*, she mouthed at him.

He laughed, but he didn't come anywhere near her as everyone else started appearing, helping Mary set out the dinner. Cash had decided to keep Izzy at their cabin and eat there, as he often did when things got a little dicey.

But Anna also had to wonder if the knowledge Chessa had been involved in all this made him less inclined to be around them. Much like she hadn't loved the idea of her family poking around her past to figure out who was after her, likely Cash didn't like being reminded of what a disaster his daughter's mother had turned out to be.

But the rest of them congregated around the table, and no one bothered with small talk tonight. They went straight into the case.

"I suppose the only positive is that if the case does go cold, we're experts at that," Palmer said, clearly trying to ease some of the tension in the room.

Jack scowled harder. Hawk set down his fork. It clearly did not have the desired effect.

"I do not plan on letting this investigation go cold. If CS Computer Systems wasn't the thread we thought it was, we only have to find a new thread. I've got some reports from all the fires. My office is chasing down potential buyers of the accelerants and fire starters used. We should have some names to check out by tomorrow."

"Should have. Check out. These aren't done deals," Louisa pointed out.

"No, they're steps in an investigation. Hart is looking into Chessa. Phone records and the like. It just takes time to get the search warrants and what have you. Tomorrow, we should have a break in the case."

"Or it's all more dead ends," Mary said. She was not usually the voice of doom, so that made Anna's heart sink.

But as she listened to them bandy about shoulds and possibilities and the word *tomorrow* more times than she cared to count, she knew... She just knew what they had to do.

"I think it's actually pretty clear what we need to do," Anna said. She knew no one would like it. Hell, she didn't like it. But it was the only way to end this. "We need to set a trap," Anna announced.

And was shocked beyond belief that Hawk had said the exact same thing in unison.

HAWK TURNED TO look at Anna. She'd said the exact same thing he had. He supposed he shouldn't be surprised. They were both investigators. Both knew how time passing made things more complicated. And she was familiar with cold cases, so she was even clearer on that.

But when she looked at him, so surprised he'd suggested the same thing, he had a very, very bad feeling. "I'm guessing our definition of *trap* is a little different."

The surprise on her face slackened into something a little more Anna-like. Not quite the snarky bravado she'd no doubt get to, but her mouth was on its way to a challenging smirk. "Yeah, I'm guessing it is."

He fought the words that bubbled up. It was no use ordering Anna to do or not to do something, but... "You aren't risking yourself, so I don't know why we'd even bother to discuss whatever you're cooking up."

Anna rolled her eyes and opened her mouth to no doubt argue, but Jack cut her off.

"I'm with Hawk. I'm sure we're all with Hawk. You're not risking yourself." He said it with authority that most people would no doubt mindlessly follow.

Except Anna. Hawk had no doubt Anna would argue until she was blue in the face, but Jack clearly knew this, too.

"Let's hear Hawk's plan. Then we'll come back to your terrible one," Jack said, then smiled blandly at her.

She narrowed her eyes at Jack, which he figured kept Anna's ire geared toward her brother rather than him, which was nice.

"I've caught up on everything today. Talked to everyone. Combed reports. We're at a brick wall, and as far as I can see, the only possible lead through that brick wall is Chessa Scott."

No one said anything. Everyone who'd been listening to him intently looked down at their plates or at the wall or beyond him. He wasn't exactly surprised by the reaction, but he didn't understand why none of them saw this as an opportunity.

"Chessa is our most connected lead. Maybe she didn't know the guy who hired her, but she's spoken with him. She knows *things* about him. If we lay a kind of trap for Chessa, she can lead us up the ladder."

"I thought Hart was looking into it," Louisa said, frowning.

"He is, but so far he's coming up empty. Chessa knows more. If we get her somewhere she feels safe to spill her guts, she can lead us in the right direction. Whether it's how she got paid or where she met the guy. *Something.* She won't talk to the police, or me, but she might talk to someone she has a connection to."

"She hates us," Mary said, and Hawk was surprised at the sharp note in Mary's usually mild tone. "She wouldn't do anything to help us. I hate to say anyone is all bad or can't be redeemed, but Chessa has been using bitterness as a weapon and an excuse since she was sixteen years old, if not longer. She's not going to help out of the goodness of her heart. In fact, she'd take every opportunity to hurt us—particularly Cash and Izzy, who she blames for the downward spiral of her life."

Hawk glanced at Anna. She was also an "especially" on Chessa's list for having stopped her from getting her hands on Izzy, but Anna was the only one who knew that. "Then we don't appeal to her heart. We appeal to the desire to hurt. To get back at you guys."

"How?"

"We use Cash as the bait. He can handle himself. We'll take precautions so she can't hurt him, but she'll think she can. And in her anger, she might let some more information go, especially since he's not law enforcement and isn't super involved in investigating."

There was a fraught silence, where all the siblings exchanged glances that spoke volumes Hawk couldn't fully read. Clearly there was more history here than he was privy to, and more of that family bond stuff he'd just never fully understand or be a part of.

"He won't go for it," Grant said, and it held weight since Grant never said much.

"Maybe not, but I think it's worth asking. Maybe he'd have an alternate plan along the same lines that he'd be more comfortable with." And maybe he'd just go for it because they *needed* to move forward. Because it was his sister at risk. The Hudsons were supposed to be about protecting one another. How could Cash not step up for this? "We cannot sit around twiddling our thumbs, and we cannot risk you," he said pointedly at Anna.

"But you can risk my brother?" she returned, her voice deceptively mild.

"It wouldn't be a risk for him. Not as much of one. Cash doesn't have your temper, and he's not going to lose his lunch if a smell hits him the wrong way." Hawk looked around the table and could not get a read on anyone's response. "We could do it carefully, safely. It's worth a shot."

Which was how Hawk found himself walking down to Cash's cabin after dinner. Hawk wasn't sure why he'd been elected to go down to Cash's cabin to approach him about the subject alone. Or maybe he knew exactly why.

They'd rather have Cash shellac an outsider than one of their own.

But Hawk could take it. And he could be persuasive. The Hudsons were loyal and protective. Why wouldn't Cash jump at the chance to protect his sister?

Pita trotted beside Hawk, his wound having healed nicely and the dog being back to his eager, puppy ways. Still, Hawk watched his surroundings. The winter sun was falling quickly, and whatever snowmelt had happened today had already iced back over.

Someone was out there…somewhere. And they wanted Anna dead. They'd been quiet for too many days now, and Hawk didn't trust it. The narrow miss with Chessa felt like a wake-up call for everyone involved.

Whatever happened next was going to be *it*, bigger and more dangerous, and Hawk was determined to be the one who came out on top. Whether the Hudsons were comfortable with his methods or not.

A few dogs trotted over to greet Pita as Hawk got closer to the cabin. He walked up onto the porch and knocked on the door, watching Pita bound and prance with the other dogs. But when the door opened, the puppy shot inside before Hawk could get out the order to stay.

Izzy was there to catch him and greet him happily. She snuggled him and laughed when he exuberantly licked her face. Hawk had to work very hard not to think about what Chessa had said about that sweet little girl.

Cash looked Hawk up and down, glanced back into the cabin where Izzy was happily cuddling Pita. "Stay inside with Pita, Izzy. Hawk and I are going to talk outside."

The little girl looked up at both of them with curiosity, but she posed no argument. Hawk had the sinking suspicion that meant she was far sneakier than she let on. But he was focused on Cash and getting through to him. Whatever Izzy found out or didn't was her business and Cash's. Not Hawk's.

Cash closed the door, keeping the two of them outside on the porch. Hawk was huddled in his jacket and felt the frigid evening air biting through. Cash stood there in a threadbare sweatshirt and looked like he was enjoying the tropics.

The Hudson men all looked alike. Big, dark hair and eyes, a kind of restrained cop-like intimidation factor. Though their personalities shone through in the way they acted, moved and spoke, put the four of them together and they were a similar wall of stoicism. Still, Cash was definitely more…fringe than Jack, Grant and Palmer. He lived apart from the main group, focused more on his daughter and his dogs than he did on investigations, and mainly kept his opinions to himself.

Which made it harder to know how to approach him. But Hawk always figured the straightforward way was best. "I need your help."

"I know what you want," Cash returned, leaning against the door as he crossed his arms over his chest. "I'm an investigator, too. Or was. I understand the wall you're at. I understand Chessa's a thread. But I'm staying out of it."

"Out of someone trying to kill your sister?"

Cash didn't even flinch, which surprised Hawk considering how close the Hudsons were. Cash stood there, a foreboding rock of *hell no.* "I've got a kid. Maybe yours isn't real to you yet, but trust me. Once that defenseless baby is on this side of the world, you would do anything, risk anything, to keep them safe. No matter how hard those choices are."

"I'm not asking you to risk Izzy." He'd die for that kid himself, and he didn't even know why.

"No, but you're asking me to risk myself. I know too well what it's like not to have parents. I can't risk that for her."

Hawk's heart twisted, though he tried to harden himself to it. He was an investigator in this instance, not an orphaned kid.

"You're asking me because you don't want Anna to do the risking," Cash continued. "I get that. I respect it and appreciate it, since it means you love her and all. But I can't be the one to step in and do it for her."

"Okay, you don't want to risk yourself. I get it. But we can agree, as two men who love her, that we don't want Anna to risk herself. What do you suggest, then? Because we can't let this case go cold. As a man who has worked on cold cases, you have to know how bad that would be."

Cash simply nodded. And said nothing.

Hawk had to work very hard to tamp down his frustration. "And your ex-wife is part of it."

"Yeah, sounds about right," Cash agreed, and then fell into another long silence.

Hawk shoved his hands into his pockets, both against the biting cold and his threadbare temper. "You have a history with Chessa. If you won't help your sister, you should at least be able to give us some insight. How do we get her to give us information? That's all I'm after, Cash."

Cash studied him coolly, as if he didn't believe him. But Hawk stood there and waited, even as the sun sank behind the mountains and the air got colder and colder.

Finally, Cash sighed. "You want insight? I don't have any. I never understood Chessa. We were kids when we got together, immature teenagers when we got married and had a kid. We weren't ready for anything life threw at us, and she decided to bemoan that fact, and I decided to deal with it—I'd had experience in that, after all. I might have felt sorry for her once, but… She wasn't just a bad mother—she was a dangerous mother. It was a relief when she finally left. I didn't understand her then—I sure as hell don't understand her now. And any connection to Chessa is an avenue into her being more drawn to causing pain and suffering. I can't risk her touching my daughter ever again. Not even to solve this case."

"If we tie her up on this, she's in jail. She's not a danger to you or Izzy."

"And if she slips through the cracks, Izzy becomes a target. My whole family becomes a target. Chessa is driven by anger, spite and the consistent belief she's been wronged. She's an addict, unpredictable at best when she's *not* on something. Forget it when she is. I don't understand anything that drives her, but I understand she's dangerous to everyone I love. So the best thing for all of us is to steer absolutely clear. I don't expect you to take my word on that, but if you ask around, ask Anna herself, you'll find they all agree."

Hawk had nothing to say to that. No smart words, no harsh demands. No easy answers. *This* was why the Hudsons had let him come down here alone, with his head of steam and self-righteousness.

You couldn't risk a kid—couldn't ask a father to risk his or her safety. Maybe he didn't understand all the fatherhood things Cash no doubt did, but he understood this. His kid wasn't even breathing yet, and he…couldn't imagine ever letting his child face any danger.

The problem was, it didn't change the issue at hand. Chessa Scott was their best bet into getting a lead.

Hawk couldn't simply let that go.

Chapter Seventeen

Anna thought about following Hawk down to Cash's cabin. She had no doubt her brother would shut down any and all talk about going through Chessa, but she also knew Hawk wouldn't give up.

And neither would she.

So when he finally came up to bed, she was ready for him. Or she thought she was. She twisted in the window seat where she'd been watching the stars. Hawk entered first. Pita pranced in behind him looking happy.

Hawk looked exhausted. Just worn down to the bone.

"He said no," Anna offered, trying to sound sympathetic without any thread of *we told you so* in her tone.

Hawk sighed. "Yeah. I guess I should have figured you guys knew him better than I did, but I just thought…" He shook his head. "Can't blame him for wanting to protect his daughter."

Anna slid off the window seat. She didn't fully cross to him. She had a feeling if she went over there and slid her arms around his neck like she wanted to, not much talking would get done, and they needed to sort this out.

Because she'd had time to think. Figure out the best way to get through the brick wall that was Hawk Steele on a mission. But she had to find some…levity. Some of her old bravado. She couldn't treat it so seriously he balked.

But she was having a hard time finding any of her old attitudes when so much felt like it was at stake. "I have a compromise."

His expression hardened and he crossed his arms over his chest as he scowled down at her. "I will not compromise on this."

She had to bite back a dreamy sigh. Even exhausted and clearly irritated with her, he was just so damn attractive. But she had to make her point before she gave in to that.

"You said it yourself—we use her hate. She hates me. I know you want to protect the baby. I get that, but you're not the only one, Hawk. You think I'm carrying around this thing for fun?" She spread her hands over her belly. She thought her pants had been a *little* tight this morning, but it was still early enough sometimes it was hard to believe it was real.

And yet she was thinking about futures and what that looked like with a baby. Worrying over them even though there was nothing to do on the outside except hope they were growing well in there. "He or she is as real to me as Izzy is."

She looked up at him under her lashes, saw the softening. There was no doubt to her that he'd be a good father. Oh, they'd no doubt butt heads on a million choices people had to make when it came to raising kids, but she knew… a safe, healthy, happy child was all he really wanted.

Because he'd lost that safety and happiness when he'd been so young. And so had she. Which made her not want to talk about Chessa or danger. She wanted… "In fact, I was thinking about names," she said.

One eyebrow winged up, and suspicion tinged his tone. "Names, huh?"

"Sure. Eagle if it's a boy. Sparrow if it's a girl."

He rolled his eyes. "Ha. Ha." But his mouth curved in amusement anyway.

She used that. That crack in his armor. That softening. She moved a little closer, reached out and took his hand. Then she placed it over her stomach. Because even with her bird name joke, she *had* been thinking about names. And it *was* serious.

"What was your mom's name?"

He stilled, kept his gaze on his hand on her stomach. She watched, and though not much in his expression or the way he held himself changed, she could *feel* the little war of emotion inside him. "Caroline."

"I like it."

"What about your mom's name?"

"Laura, but… How about this? Girl, we go with Caroline Laura Hudson-Steele. Boy, we go with my dad's name, Dean, and a middle name you think your mom would have liked. What about Hawk? Like a family heirloom. Pass it on down."

He was quiet and very still for a long moment. When he spoke, his voice was rough. "Yeah, that sounds good."

She had to fight a wave of tears. Happy tears, but she didn't want them falling. She wanted to be strong. "It does, doesn't it?"

His blue eyes lifted to hers. A million emotions swirled there, but he kept them carefully controlled. "Anna, I can't… It's too much to lose. I knew that already, but everything Cash said made it…clearer."

"I know." Talking about names made it clearer, too. All

the things she *wanted* to do, the way she'd normally act. But things weren't normal anymore. She had to be someone different than she'd once been. "But we can't just… wait it out. We both know that."

Hawk nodded.

"What if the two of us went to the jail? I know Jack won't like it. Hart probably won't either. But we find a way to talk to her there, a way to…get something out of her. Where it's safe. And you'll be with me, okay? We won't tackle anything alone. Chessa is dangerous because she's unpredictable and connected in ways we don't understand, but she isn't loyal to that guy. Jack and Hart aren't getting anywhere because she knows not to trust the cops, *and* she doesn't hate them. Personally. She hates me. Personally. She won't *want* to tell me anything, sure. But if we rile her up, use her anger and her hate, she might slip."

"And if she doesn't?" Hawk asked.

Anna wished she had anything smart to say. Or encouraging. Or anything. But all she had in this moment was the honest truth. "I don't know, but we just keep trying."

HAWK DIDN'T SLEEP WELL. There was too much on his mind. Anna's plan wasn't terrible; it was just unlikely to yield results.

Desperation caused mistakes, and if this was a normal investigation, he'd carefully and methodically be pulling the threads. But nothing felt normal because it all involved the woman he'd fallen in love with.

He watched the light begin to dawn in the window, while Anna slept soundly beside him, Pita down at the foot of the bed.

Terrifying thing, being happy. Knowing how tenuous

it all was even without someone wanting Anna dead. All the worse with this cloud hanging over their lives.

And sitting here thinking about it didn't solve that cloud, did it? He slid out of bed, trying not to wake either bedmate, but Pita lifted his head and let out a little whimper. Hawk scooped him up so as not to disturb Anna and grabbed some clothes with his other hand.

He put Pita down in the hallway. "You sit tight," he ordered the dog. He stepped into the bathroom and got dressed. When he came back out, Pita was still sitting there, his little tail wagging. Hawk crouched down and gave the dog a good scratch behind the ears. "You're the best little boy, aren't you?" he murmured at the dog.

"Maybe tied for best."

Hawk looked up to see Anna standing in her bedroom doorway, sleep-disheveled and gorgeous, with that little smirk on her face that tended to make his brain short-circuit.

"Remember how you didn't want a dog?" she asked, tapping her chin. "But Mary walked you right into a corner."

He got to his feet. "Yeah, yeah." He was about to pull her to him when someone's door opened down the hall. A creak, followed by footsteps. A loud yawn.

"Morning," Palmer offered, sliding past them and then to the bathroom.

There were more noises now. The sounds of people chatting, walking. Something clattered downstairs. Her whole family getting ready to start the day. She wanted to live here, and he didn't care where he lived, but damn, he could use a *little* privacy. "When you said you wanted to live here, did you mean in this exact bedroom?"

She smiled. "We each have our own little parcel of land. Palmer's building Louisa a house on his for when they get married. I guess I figured that's what I'd do if I ever found myself ball-and-chained to a man."

"Speaking of that, when are we going to get ball-and-chained? I've got a friend who's a judge. No waiting in Wyoming, you know."

She narrowed her eyes at him—and maybe he'd been expecting that, hoping for that. "There is no big fat rock on my finger, and I am not getting married by a *judge*. There will be a wedding, a white dress, the whole shebang."

"When?"

She all-out scowled now.

"I know you keep thinking you might yet scare me off, Blondie," he said, tapping that scowl. "But I won't shake."

She moved forward, wrapped her arms around his neck and pressed her mouth to his. "Then buy me a rock, Steele." Then she kissed him again.

Until they were interrupted by a disgusted groan. "Your room is *right there*," Palmer said, gesturing at the open door as he passed again, this time to go to the stairs. He muttered darkly under his breath as he disappeared.

But before either of them could say anything else, Jack appeared at the top of the stairs. Considering *his* bedroom was downstairs, and he immediately turned toward their side of the hall, Hawk had a bad feeling.

Anna tensing in his arms added to it. Hawk didn't see anything different about Jack—all stoic expressions and ramrod postures—but still knew the bad news was coming.

And Jack got right to it as he approached them—not even one comment about their arms around each other.

"I just got off the phone with one of my deputies. Someone paid Chessa's bail. She got out early this morning. An hour or two before anyone told me."

"How?" Hawk demanded, at the same time Anna said about the same thing.

"How does that happen, Jack?"

They didn't let each other go precisely, but they turned to face Jack, Hawk's arm around her shoulders, Anna holding on to his side.

Jack shook his head. "I'm on my way to the station to find out. I want you two to stay—"

"I'm coming with," Hawk said, effectively cutting Jack off. He let Anna go and stepped forward. "You, me, Hart, we get to the bottom of this to triangulate our investigations. Grant's here, right?"

"You might be the arson investigator, Steele, but you don't have jurisdiction over me," Jack returned, not answering his question.

"I don't give a rat's ass about jurisdiction. I either go with you or I follow you and bust my way in. It doesn't matter to me. Now, is Grant here? Is Palmer sticking around?" He pointed at Anna behind him, who was being uncharacteristically quiet. "Someone to keep an eye on her."

"Grant and Dahlia are visiting her sister out of town until tonight. Palmer will stick around, and I'll leave it to Mary to update everyone on what's going on. I—"

"What about Cash?" Anna interrupted, without even chastising him for the "someone to keep an eye on her" comment. "If Chessa is—"

"I already warned him," Jack said, clearly gentling his tone for Anna. "He's decided to stay put at the cabin, locked up tight with the dogs, until she's found."

"Then let's go. Anna, you'll stay here. Never alone. Not until we figure out what's going on," Jack said. Ordered.

Hawk turned to Anna. She mounted no argument, and she didn't even have that look on her face like she was planning something devious or rebellious.

"You're being…not yourself."

She looked up at him, hazel eyes a maze of conflicting emotions. "You'll be with my brother." She looked over Hawk's shoulder to where Jack stood. Held her brother's gaze. "I'd trust him with my life, so I'll trust him with yours."

Hawk pulled her into a quick hug. "Nice guilt trip, Blondie." He kissed her cheek, then looked her in the eye. "Be safe."

She stared at him for a long time. "We split up last time and it didn't work."

"We're not splitting up. I'm with Jack and Hart. You're with Palmer and Mary. No one goes it alone. Deal?"

She looked up at him, and it worried him he couldn't read her expression. But she got up on her toes and brushed her mouth over his. "Deal."

Chapter Eighteen

Anna didn't like feeling shaken, but something about Chessa getting out of jail shattered whatever small amount of peace she'd been able to thread together since Hawk had been hurt.

Anna wished she could believe Chessa would disappear. Take some money and run. But someone had gotten her out of jail, which meant someone was still using her.

Someone. Someone that no one—not herself, when she'd always considered herself an above-average investigator, not her siblings who she'd always viewed as the same, not Hawk—no one could find out who wanted Anna dead.

But Hawk was with Jack. She trusted her brother, *had* to trust him, to keep Hawk out of harm's way. And vice versa.

So she sat at the breakfast table with Mary and Palmer. Grant had stayed at Dahlia's last night since Dahlia had her monthly visit to her sister's. Palmer had insisted Louisa stay with her family until things settled a little.

"So, since you can't stop making out with the guy in our damn hallway, I guess you're going to marry him?" Palmer asked casually, sipping his coffee.

Anna knew he was trying to keep her mind off everything else. She wanted to play along, but she felt wound too tight. Too ready to snap.

"What's the security situation?" she asked.

Palmer sighed, but he didn't put her off. "We've found a solution for the breach, but I don't think we can rely on it the way we usually would. Someone who can create one breach can always create another."

"And no one can find anything incriminating on this CS Computer Systems?"

"You've looked into it just like the rest of us, Anna. If it's a connection, we can't find it. And we can't focus on *one* thing just because it seems more likely, when we're not getting anywhere."

Anna knew all these things. Had probably said these things to frustrated people wanting answers. Now she was on the other side of it, now it was *her* life and… She wanted to go back in time and punch herself in the face. What an awful person she'd been to people in desperate need of answers.

No wonder someone wanted her dead.

"Anna," Palmer said, so sternly he almost sounded like Jack. "It feels different when it's personal. When you're trying to keep people you love safe. That's why we've got people like Hart working on the case, too. You need people who don't have a connection. Who can have that patience we don't have."

"All we can do is keep working," Mary said calmly. "It's what we always do. And it doesn't really matter what we *feel* while we do them, does it? Cold case or new case. You or Louisa or Hawk are victims, or someone we've never met is, we just have to keep connecting the dots. And weathering the storms that crop up while we do."

Anna looked at her sister. She sounded so in control. She always did. Jack, Grant and Mary. Always made it seem like everything was possible. They'd been the back-bone after Mom and Dad had disappeared. In the midst of questions that had never been answered, Jack had waded through the financial realities of the ranch, while Cash had taken on the actual labor of it all. Mary had shoul-dered the administrative tasks to keep the household run-ning, even though she'd only been ten years old, and Grant had driven them to and from school. Checked homework.

All Anna had ever done was be the baby of the fam-ily. The one everyone took care of. Even now. What was she doing besides waiting around for someone to solve this case for her?

The landline rang and Mary went to answer it. Her pleasant business smile faded, and she dropped the phone, already running for the back door. "Cash's cabin is on fire. They can't get out."

They all headed toward the door, but Anna and Palmer stopped. Anna looked out the window. She could see the smoke off in the distance. But the fires so far had been warnings. This one wasn't just a warning.

It was likely a trap.

"Mary, don't!" Anna yelled at the same time Palmer did, but Mary had opened the door. She'd only taken a step before a gunshot rang out.

Mary stumbled back as Palmer grabbed her and pulled her out of the doorway. Anna dropped to the ground as another shot rang out, exploding through the window. She crawled over to Mary and Palmer.

"Don't look at it," Palmer ordered, because everyone knew Mary hated the sight of blood. And her arm was bloody. Just her arm. Just her arm.

Anna repeated that to herself as she ripped Mary's torn

sleeve out of the way. Palmer handed her a dish towel and Anna pressed it to where Mary was bleeding.

"Call Jack," Anna said to Palmer.

"You two stay put and call him. I'm going."

Anna grabbed on to Palmer with one hand, while she pressed the bandage to Mary's arm with the other. "You can't go out there alone."

"We can't wait for emergency services to get all the way out here. Cash and Izzy are trapped."

"They're stuck in the house, Anna," Mary said. "You both have to go get them out. I'm okay."

"Not with people shooting," Anna returned. "We have to be smarter than that." And she *was* smarter. She had to stop reacting and actually think. Actually *act*. She took Mary's hand and had her wrap the cloth around her own wound. "Can you hold that there? Keep the pressure?"

Mary swallowed and nodded. She was beyond pale.

"I know you hate blood, so just don't look. Just hold on. Okay?"

Mary nodded, though Anna was concerned it was more of a panic nod than actual understanding. "I'm okay. I'm okay…" she stammered. "Don't worry about me. Get Cash and Izzy."

Anna turned to Palmer and looked at his gun. Cash had guns locked up in his cabin, and hopefully had been smart enough to grab one. They had some back in the security room, but it would take too long to get them. They needed to act now.

"Give me the gun," she ordered Palmer.

He hesitated, but only for a second. She unlocked the safety, positioned herself next to the window. She had a hole to shoot through, and a good view of the field between the big house and Cash's cabin where the smoke was coming from. She couldn't find the gunman. Yet. But she would.

"I'll cover you," Anna said to Palmer, though her gaze never left the area around the fire, searching for a shooter. "If there's more than two gunmen, you come right back. If there's one or two, I'll take them out, and you get to Cash and Izzy." She moved her gaze from outside to Palmer. "Got it?"

He gave a short nod. Then Anna looked out the window, pointed the gun in the most likely direction of one shooter and pulled the trigger just as Palmer took off toward the smoke.

HAWK DROVE HIS own truck and followed Jack to the Sunrise jail where Chessa had been held. Pita sat happily in the passenger seat, watching the snowy world go by. Hawk parked next to Jack when he pulled to a stop in front of the small building that housed the sheriff's department.

Hawk got out and grabbed Pita's leash, letting the dog jump out on his own. The puppy didn't do his usual sniffing around. He followed Jack as if he knew this was all serious business.

Hawk didn't have to be a mind reader or a psychologist to know that Jack Hudson's mood was foul. It radiated off the man as he strode inside the building—even before he started barking out orders to his staff.

It was interesting to watch the deputies and administrative assistants jump to do exactly what he said. No shared looks of irritation or hesitation. If Jack was a hard-ass, he was at least a respected hard-ass here.

Hawk had to appreciate it. He tried to allow the quick, helpful reactions to give him some hope that they could figure out what had happened with Chessa.

A young woman in a police uniform strode up to them. "Ferguson is the one who took care of it. He's over at City Hall right now. Should I go get him?"

"Yeah. Make sure he brings a copy of the receipt or the ID."

The woman nodded, then strode past, though she did flash the puppy a little smile as she did.

Jack looked at an elderly woman behind a big desk. "When Brink gets back with Ferguson, have them come to my office. In the meantime, make sure Kinsey sends the video surveillance directly to my email. No one else. Understood?"

"Yes, sir," she said, then handed Hawk a dog treat. "Always keep these on hand for our four-legged helpers."

Hawk thanked the woman, then tossed Pita the treat. Jack jerked a chin at Hawk, as if to say *follow me*, but they both stopped short when Hart marched in. Hawk had never seen the detective look quite so angry.

"How does this happen?" Hart demanded of Jack. "She was my one lead."

"She was *our* one lead on the attack on my *sister's* life, so spare me your outrage," Jack returned. "We're questioning the officer who took the bond. We won't all fit, but let's head back to my office."

Jack led them back into a tiny room, barely the size of a closet. He strode inside, set his keys and hat down on the desk. A cat figure-eighted around one of the legs of the chair.

Hawk and Hart exchanged glances. Even one of them

would be a tight fit, so they both wordlessly agreed to hover in the doorway.

"Maybe this isn't a disaster," Hawk suggested. "Maybe it could be a lead. She had a decent-sized bond. Whoever paid her way has means. It's got to be our guy, or she wouldn't have needed the payout in the first place."

"Maybe it is, but I doubt it. At best, he sent an intermediary. At worst, Chessa's dead and *all* our leads are gone."

Hawk looked from Jack to Hart. "That your read?"

"Look, we've got a guy willing to kill Anna. I don't know why he'd worry about killing anyone else, and if he thinks Chessa has information? It adds up. Maybe. Certainly a possibility we can't rule out."

Hawk didn't say anything. If whoever had bailed Chessa out was the man who'd been trying to kill Anna, who'd bashed him over the head and hurt Pita in the process, he was certainly capable of killing Chessa to make sure she didn't talk.

But Chessa hadn't been talking. There'd been no name. No connection. Bailing her out to use her again seemed far more likely in Hawk's mind, which meant he was going to view this as a lead.

It had to be a lead.

Eventually, the female officer returned with a young man who looked pale and nervous. Hawk watched him carefully.

"Tell us about last night."

"Sir?"

"Chessa Scott. Someone bailed her out. I want to know how it went down."

"Oh, uh." The kid—Ferguson—looked around at Hart, then Hawk, then at the female officer. Brink, Jack had called her. "Um. Well, he came in. Said he wanted to pay Chessa Scott's bail."

"Did you take his ID?"

The man—*boy*—blinked. "What?"

"Did you take the damn ID, Ferguson?"

"Y-yes, sir. I followed the protocol."

"And?"

"I don't... I'd have to go look at the records."

Jack rubbed his hands over his face. Hawk wondered if the man would have an aneurysm right there, but the female officer from before held out a binder. "Here's the book."

"Ferguson, find me the receipt and tell me anything else you remember."

Ferguson nodded, taking the binder with shaky hands. Hawk exchanged a look with Hart as if to say *who hired this guy?*

Ferguson cleared his throat. "He didn't say much. When I let Ms. Scott go, she said he was her boyfriend, then kind of laughed a bunch."

"Did he argue with her? Act like he was?" Jack demanded.

With shaking hands, Ferguson pulled out a piece of paper. He handed it to Jack. "Neither. He just kind of dragged her out of here. He had the money. Everything was on the up-and-up. I didn't do anything wrong." The kid looked around wildly. "I followed directions and—"

Jack silenced him with a sharp look as he took the receipt. But that look chilled considerably as he looked down at the receipt. Hawk's nerves began to hum.

"Hawk? Go back to the ranch," Jack said, his voice cold and detached as he handed the receipt to Hart.

"What? Why?" Hawk demanded, thinking he was

being shuttled off for some obnoxious Hudson protection reason that he'd never begin to understand.

Then he saw the cold fury on Jack's face as Jack grabbed his keys and slid his hat back on his head. "It was one of my ranch hands."

Chapter Nineteen

As Palmer ran, Anna shot. She caught a glimpse of one shooter and focused all her fire there. After a few shots, she was almost certain he was the only gunman. But she was having a hard time getting the right angle to take him out.

Which left Palmer way too out in the open as gunfire echoed through the otherwise calm Wyoming winter morning.

Anna wanted to look at Mary and make sure she was doing okay, but she couldn't take her eyes off her target. She couldn't stop focusing her shooting toward the person who might shoot Palmer.

Then she caught it. The little flash. The gunman moving just enough into range she pulled the trigger and watched as the man jerked. She didn't even hear the explosion of the gunshot. It didn't matter. Nothing mattered except that she'd hit him.

"I got the shooter. I'm going after Palmer."

"Anna—"

"Stay put. Wait for help," Anna called over her shoulder. She didn't know if Mary would listen—probably only if she wasn't capable of walking. But Anna had to get over to where all that smoke plumed in the bright blue sky.

She wasn't foolish enough not to be careful. She eyed

her surroundings, the horizon, as she jogged toward the cabin, toward Palmer. She kept the gun in her hand. She'd shoot anyone who got in her way.

She didn't see signs of anyone else. It would be reckless for one gunman to think he could take on all the Hudsons living here, but maybe he'd assumed the fire would panic them.

Or maybe there's more coming.

Maybe, but she had to focus on Cash and Izzy in this moment. She reached Palmer just as he'd made it to the window Cash had clearly broken from the inside. Cash was working from the inside, Palmer from the outside to pull Izzy out. Once Palmer had her, he passed her to Anna so he could help Cash.

The girl was getting far too big for Anna to carry, and Izzy was coughing up a storm. So Anna half carried, half dragged her away from the burning house.

"Daddy," Izzy croaked.

"He's coming, sweetie. You're both okay." Anna surveyed the landscape. Mary was scurrying across the yard, towel still clamped to her arm. She came up to Izzy and wrapped her arm around the girl. "Come on. Let's get you into the house."

Izzy was crying now. "Daddy. I want Daddy."

"He's coming," Anna assured her as Palmer helped Cash away from the house. Cash's face was streaked with sweat and smoke, and he was coughing, too. He wasn't limping, but he seemed to need Palmer's support to walk.

Anna looked around. Where the hell was help? She needed someone to track down the shooter she'd shot in case he hadn't been shot that badly and came back.

Mary was cradling Izzy, but she pushed away from

Mary—causing Mary to gasp in pain—as Cash approached. Izzy threw her arms around her father.

"I'm okay," Cash rasped. "You need to get inside, sweets."

"The fire trucks and ambulance should be here any minute. Any minute," Mary said, repeating it over and over again, like that would make it so as they trudged toward the house.

But the shooter was still out there. Everyone here was safe from the fire, though needing medical attention. Anna watched their surroundings as they clambered onto the back porch.

They could barricade themselves inside, but it would be another loose end, another question mark. Anna had to find the gunman and make sure he was down and identified. That he couldn't come back. That this *ended*.

She pulled Palmer aside. "I've got to make sure he's down."

"Not alone, Anna."

"He's alone. I've got a gun and I'm not shot like he is. Keep an eye on these three. They're hurt and they'll need someone to flag down the EMTs." Someone to stay, and Anna wasn't any good at comforting.

Besides, this was *her* fight.

So she didn't bother to argue with Palmer. She took off. She couldn't let the guy get away. She hadn't seen him enough to ID him. They needed a lead. They needed to find out who was terrorizing them. All because of her.

She ran toward the spot where he'd been when she shot him and was gratified he hadn't gone far. There was a trail of blood in the snow, and then a man crawling away. Slowly. Haltingly.

But Anna recognized this man. It made her steps falter. "Tripp?"

The man looked back over his shoulder at her. Then his eyes widened at the gun in her hand. He stumbled a bit, so he fell on his back, and she could see she'd shot him in the stomach. He was bleeding badly.

Tripp. One of their ranch hands. She didn't want to believe it of him—she'd herded cattle with him, she'd *joked* with him just last Christmas when they'd passed out the Christmas presents. He'd been a trusted member of their team.

And he'd done *this*? She pointed the gun at him. Right between the eyes, anger and shame making a dangerous storm within her. Because how *dare* he?

What the hell might she have done to make him want to kill her? "What do you have to say for yourself?" she asked. Her voice shook, but her hands on the gun didn't.

Tripp's eyes were wide and wild. He held up his hands in a kind of surrender as he kicked his legs against the ground like he could scoot away. Blood oozed from his torn shirt. "I..."

But then she heard a gun cock, right behind her. The cold press of steel to her temple.

"Don't move," the low voice ordered.

Anna did as she was told. She held herself very still. Using only peripheral vision, she looked around and tried to spot any of her family members.

But she'd fallen into a trap, hadn't she? She'd been foolish enough, angry enough, to leave herself vulnerable. Always her downfall.

"You know the worst part of this whole thing?" she

said, imbuing her voice with all the old casual bravado she didn't even remotely feel.

"That you're going to end up dead?"

"No, that I don't even know *why*. I don't know who the hell you are, pal. So whatever number I did on you, I don't remember. I don't know which one of us that makes more pathetic. Maybe both."

"You think this is about you?" The man laughed, his breath hot on her neck. "You would. You're all a bunch of selfish, self-absorbed criminals. And you're all going to pay. You had to make it more difficult. You had to make me angrier. Now it won't just be blame they're heaping on themselves. They're all going to watch you die."

HAWK SLAMMED ON his brakes as he approached the Hudson house, one hand on the wheel, one arm around Pita.

He saw it in the distance: smoke. Fire. Not at the main house. *Hell.* Cash's cabin.

There was no way his car would make it over the drifts of snow, so he got out and he ran. Pita must have jumped out of the driver's side behind him because the dog was right next to him, racing toward the danger. There was no time to tell him to stop.

Hawk's chest constricted as he got close. Fire consumed the cabin. If anyone was in there... No, surely—

He saw tracks leading to and from it. Clearly people had run back and forth. As he got closer, he could see the front window had been broken. They'd gotten out.

But someone had barricaded the door shut. Hawk tried to ice away the cold fury that swept over him. He had to think clearly. Carefully.

They'd gotten out, which meant everyone would be back

at the main house. So Hawk ran for the house, where the tracks led, Pita still by his side. The back door was open, and Mary, Cash and Izzy were just inside in various states of disarray.

But no Anna.

Mary was holding something to her arm, and Izzy was coughing. Cash stood there abnormally still, like he was hurt but was trying not to let on. Hawk didn't see Palmer or Anna, so they had to be together. Which was good. He could relax.

He could not relax.

"Where's help?" Cash demanded when Hawk jogged up the porch stairs, Pita wriggling past him to go lick Izzy's face where she sat on the floor, leaning against Cash's leg.

"When did you call it in?" Hawk asked, because they hadn't gotten word of it at the police department.

"Too long ago," Mary said. "They should be here."

But he knew how time could stretch out and seem longer when everything was terrible. "We must have left before the call came through. Jack just found out it was one of your ranch hands who bailed out Chessa, so he sent me out here."

"One of the..." Mary trailed off, looked at Cash. His face was covered in grime, but as far as Hawk could tell, his expression didn't change from one of grim acceptance.

"What happened to you?" Hawk demanded, seeing the trail of blood seeping out from under the towel Mary held on her arm.

"Shot."

"Shot?" It was dumb to repeat what she'd said, but he was honestly so shocked he didn't know how to comprehend the word. Mary, of all people, being shot, when there was a fire raging, did not compute.

If there had been shooting…

"The fire was first," Mary said, as if reciting math facts. She didn't look at Hawk or Cash now. She stared at a wall. "Cash called the house because they couldn't get out. I ran out, foolishly, and someone shot at us."

Hawk's body went cold. Not just a fire. A whole damn setup. "Where's Anna?"

"She took out the gunman," Cash said, in a similarly detached voice as Mary. "Which allowed Palmer to help get Izzy and me out the window. Then Anna didn't think the gunman was dead, so she was going to find him. Palmer went after her. She's not alone, and the person they're after is hurt. They should be fine."

Well, that was some kind of relief, but he wouldn't be able to fully relax until he saw her. Because *should be* fine didn't necessarily mean much in this whole mess of a case.

They all heard the sirens then and, as if a unit, turned toward the sound. The trio here were too injured, too worn down. Hawk wanted to find Anna, but… She was with Palmer. They could handle it. "I'll grab the EMTs, tell them you're in here."

Cash nodded. Hawk looked down at the dog. "Stay," he ordered. Pita wagged his tail in Izzy's lap. Then Hawk took off toward the emergency vehicles.

As he approached, Jack was already leading the fray.

"Call came through my radio when I was on my way, but they caught up quick," Jack said as Hawk approached. "Everyone's all right?"

"More or less," Hawk returned. He gestured at the ambulance crew. "Follow me."

As he led the EMTs, Hawk relayed what Mary had said to Jack, noting the hitch in Jack's step even as nothing showed on his face. But as the house came into view, Hawk stopped and turned to Jack.

"I'm going to track down Anna and Palmer. I don't like them being out there on their own."

"No, I don't either. But you need someone with you. Best to travel in pairs."

"I'll catch up with them and then we'll be a trio. I think they'd all be glad to have you in there," Hawk said, nodding toward the house.

Jack turned behind them. "Hart?" Jack barked, and waved the detective over.

Jack was ordering him about before he'd even fully come to a stop.

"Go with Hawk here," Jack said. "There was a gunman on the property. Anna and Palmer might have taken care of him, but let's make sure."

Hawk saw a flicker of irritation cross Hart's face—since Jack was neither his boss nor his superior officer, and not even that many years older, if any, no doubt—but he didn't argue. He nodded. "All right."

Hawk might have felt some sympathy for the man on getting caught up in something where everyone wanted to be in charge, but he was too intent on finding Anna to care about much else.

"Everyone seems to think there was only one gunman, and Anna took him out, but I haven't seen a gunman, Anna *or* Palmer since I got here."

Hart nodded as they walked across the snowy ground. There were secondary tracks leading away from both house and cabin, and Hawk figured those were the best to follow. If someone had shot Mary going out the back door, it made more sense it was in this direction rather than closer to the front of the property, where emergency personnel now swarmed.

Behind a tree, triangulated to have a good view of the back door *and* the cabin that was on fire, the tracks—Anna's smaller prints, and then no doubt Palmer's larger ones obscuring some as if he came in after her—led to a little pile of snow, as if the gunman had built up a snow cover for himself. Behind the snow, streaks of blood were garish against the white.

The blood led, dripping and smearing, around the fence line. Almost like it was making a big circle around the house—toward the front. The cars maybe? Was the gunman trying to get to an escape vehicle and Anna and Palmer had followed at a distance?

Hawk scanned the horizon, but he saw no one. He glanced at Hart, who'd drawn his weapon as he surveyed the landscape around them.

"We better follow it," Hawk said, focusing on that step, rather than what might lie beyond it. Clearly the shooter was hurt, so wherever Anna and Palmer had disappeared, it was no doubt just tracking the guy. That was all they were doing. To ensure he didn't get away.

It had to be.

Chapter Twenty

Anna was led in a wide circle around her home, the gun constantly pressed to her head. The man she'd shot, their own damn ranch hand, limped and crawled and moaned behind them, but he followed.

"The fire trucks will park more toward the cabin. We should be able to get in the mudroom door without anyone seeing us," Tripp said.

Anna tried to whip her head around to glare at him, but the man with the gun to her head had wrapped his hands into her hair and painfully kept her looking straight ahead.

Anger, fury, outrage swamped her, even with the gun pressed to her head, but she tried to breathe past it. *Think.* They wanted to go into the house? What the hell was this guy after?

"We want to make sure the sheriff has joined us," the gunman said. "So we'll wait for the sirens."

But he still pushed her forward, until they were in the little line of evergreen trees her great-grandmother had planted before she was born. It gave them cover from anyone who might look out from the house.

She could make a run for it, and she would have if she wasn't pregnant. She would have risked getting shot for getting away.

But she couldn't risk her baby.

So she had to be smart—instead of smart-mouthed and impetuous, which was what usually got her through a dangerous situation.

They wanted Jack—that was what he meant by waiting for the sheriff. Because this wasn't about her. But then, why was she the target? It didn't make any sense. She tried to think of what the man said. That they'd all pay. That they'd watch her die.

It had to be about Hudson Sibling Solutions, then. There was no other explanation. "So, what, we didn't solve your cold case and now you want us dead? Way to go. That's a rational response."

Okay, maybe she'd always use her smart mouth whether *that* was smart or not.

"You're sure a mouthy one. Makes me feel less badly about choosing you. I thought about the uppity secretary. Figured she'd be the easiest target, but I want her to pay, too. You're the only one who wasn't involved, so you get to be the victim. Aren't you lucky?"

Anna let out a low whistle. "Have you considered therapy, bud? Because this is beyond messed up. It's not even rational revenge. Have you thought about meditation? Getting a puppy? Maybe solving whatever cold case yourself instead of blaming everyone else?"

"Would you shut her up?" the man demanded of Tripp.

"No one can shut her up," Tripp muttered darkly.

She smirked at Tripp, who was looking like he might pass out at any minute. He was pressing his hand to his gunshot wound, but he'd had no help. The guy holding a gun to her head hadn't even offered him some compression for the wound.

"If you die, Tripp, I won't waste one ounce of guilt on being the one who killed you. Traitorous bastard."

The man pressed the gun harder into her head, making Anna's heart flutter—though she told herself he wanted to kill her in front of everyone, which meant she had time to escape. She had time to figure her way out of this.

She had to keep telling herself that. She couldn't just die here. She couldn't. There was too much to live for.

"You won't be alive to feel guilt," the gunman said, shaking her roughly as if that would get her to stop talking.

But sirens sounded in the distance, and that did the trick. Help was on the way. She only had to make it until those sirens got here. Then if she ran, there'd be people to help. She couldn't risk her baby, but if help was nearby…

The gunman pushed her forward so hard, she nearly fell. Which would have given her the opportunity to fight without the gun pressed to her temple, but he caught her by the arm at the last second, gun still pointed right at her head.

She wanted to swear, or fight, but she forced herself to remain still. To be pushed forward toward the side door. She had to be careful, more careful than she'd ever been. For her family and her baby.

Something thudded to the ground. Both the gunman and Anna looked back. Tripp had collapsed into a heap in the snow.

The man looked down at Tripp with some disgust. Then simply shrugged. "Don't need him anymore anyway." With no warning, he reared back and kicked the mudroom door. It splintered, gave, but didn't fully open. Anna thought about running. He still had the gun pointed at her, but with the second kick, his attention would be focused on the door.

But her family was inside. She might be the target, the one he wanted to kill to hurt them, but he was clearly unhinged enough to kill anyone. And Izzy was in there. What if he decided she was a better target?

Anna's blood ran cold at the thought, so she stayed put while he finished kicking the door open. He gestured her inside with the gun. "Take me to that fancy room where you lie to people and tell them you'll find their lost loved ones. Where you take their money and lie and lie and lie."

Anna sucked in a breath. He wanted her to take him to the living room. Where they tried to make clients feel at home, taken care of. Because they knew the emotional toll of a cold case, of having *no* answers and still having that sliver of hope that answers might be out there.

He had to be a former client, but why hadn't his case stuck out to them? He wasn't Clarence Samuels—the case she'd been away in the rodeo for. He wasn't the man she'd been following when she'd been attacked.

It had to go back further than that. Not just a case she hadn't been involved in, a case before she'd been involved. Jack had started HSS when she'd only been fifteen. She hadn't been allowed to help then.

It had to be a case that far back. She wished she had any way to get that information to Jack. To Hawk. To *anyone*. But she could only walk this man through her family's home and pray they figured this out before something went terribly wrong.

She stepped into the living room. Where she'd watched cartoons on Saturday mornings before her parents had disappeared. Where she'd gotten into a rage of a fight with

Jack over wanting to go to the rodeo, and Palmer had stepped in and smoothed things over. Where she, Mary and Louisa had giggled over boys and first times. Where she'd cried in relief when Grant had come home from deployment. Where she'd walked baby Izzy in circles while Cash slept on the couch because sometimes only Aunt Anna had the right touch to get her to sleep.

Which made her think of her own baby. She didn't bring her hands to her stomach, though she wanted to. *I will do anything to protect you.* It was the only vow she knew how to make.

"No one's here," she offered to the gunman.

"You don't say," the gunman replied. "Yell for them."

Anna hesitated, which earned her a painful jab of the gun into her temple again. She winced.

"Jack?" She tried to sound…different as she called for her brother. Anything to give him a hint all was not right. Afraid, but not hurt. Shaky but not so shaky he'd come running without thinking. "Can you come into the living room? Please?" she added, because *please* wasn't in her normal arsenal.

Please read into that.

She was relieved when no thunder of footsteps started. Instead, Jack slowly entered the living room from the dining room, gun drawn.

But he stopped on a dime when he caught sight of her with a gun pressed to her head. Cash and Mary had appeared behind him, Cash with a gun of his own, Mary and Izzy holding on to each other.

"Drop the guns," the gunman ordered

Jack stilled, that cop look immediately taking over his face. Cash shoved Izzy behind Mary and Mary paled even more than she already had. But Palmer didn't appear. Where was Palmer?

"Now. Or I pull the trigger."

Jack and Cash carefully crouched, placing their guns on the ground, their gazes never leaving the gun on Anna's head.

"Kick them over here."

They did as they were told. So that they stood in a kind of standoff, the family couch between them. No one spoke. They just did what the gunman said, and Anna couldn't meet their gazes. She might break apart.

She had to find a way to get out of this situation, without dying. Without anyone she loved getting hurt.

"Hello," the gunman said, suddenly pleasant. "Remember me?"

No one said anything. Anna saw similar looks of confusion on everyone's face—except Mary.

"You're Darrin Monroe," Mary said calmly. She had her hands clasped behind her, on Izzy's shoulders as if to make sure she was always a shield.

Anna didn't recognize the name, but she could tell Jack did.

"You were one of our first cases," Jack said grimly.

"Yes, and you *failed* me. I want you all here. All of you. For every minute you're not all here, I'll make her death that much more gruesome," he said, shoving the gun hard against Anna's skull as if to prove the point. "Grant and Palmer are missing. I want them here."

"Grant is out of town. I can call Palmer, if you'd like," Mary said calmly, as if she was talking to any client they took on. Offering coffee or a place to stay.

"Yes," Darrin said. "Get Palmer here. We can do this without the other one. He wasn't part of it anyway."

"I thought I was the only one not a part of it?" Anna couldn't help but say to her captor. "Wait, I get it. You're afraid the ex-soldier could kick your ass, but the young woman wasn't a threat to you?"

"That's right. And I was correct, wasn't I?"

Well, unfortunately, she didn't have anything to say to *that*.

"We didn't fail you, Mr. Monroe," Cash said. "We found your son."

"Dead. You found him *dead*. And you were meant to find your sister dead, and never know how or why, but she just couldn't die. So now you'll watch her die. All of you. I want Palmer here, *now*."

HAWK AND HART followed the trail of blood around to the other side of the house. The man shot had clearly hidden here behind the trees for a while because there was a bigger pile of blood. Hawk peered through the trees.

Then he saw a man's body crumpled next to a broken-in door. Fear and worry twined inside him, but he pointed at the body without saying anything. Hart nodded and they moved forward as a unit, both with guns drawn. They arrived at the crumpled body and Hart crouched next to it, checking the man's pulse.

Hart looked up. "Not dead, but nearly."

"Take him to the ambulance."

Hart stood, disapproval waving off him. "Something bad is going on, Steele. You shouldn't go in there alone."

"I'm not," he said, gesturing at the broken open door. "Palmer's right there." Palmer didn't look back at them, his attention on whatever was going on inside the house. Hawk could only hope like hell Anna was safe somewhere beyond what he could see.

"I'm not taking him," Hart muttered. "I'm calling for an EMT. I'll stay here with the body, but I'm coming in after you once he's gone."

Hawk nodded, then stepped inside the mudroom. Palmer spared him only the flicker of a glance and put a finger to his lips in a *be quiet* gesture. Hawk moved forward silently to where Palmer stood. As far as he could tell, there was nothing to see but the long empty hallway.

Once Hawk was close enough, Palmer spoke in a low whisper. "He's got Anna."

Hawk didn't hear the rest of it at first. His head was a buzzing mass of static and panic. But he didn't move. He didn't yell and break things like he immediately wanted to. He breathed and pushed the thought of Anna and their baby as far out of his mind as he could.

"Who has Anna?" Hawk asked, quietly. Calmly. Maybe.

"Some guy. He popped up out of nowhere. I don't know who the hell he is, but he said he wanted to kill her in front of all the siblings to make us Hudsons pay. I followed at a distance. He doesn't know I'm here, but there hasn't been a chance to safely jump in. He's keeping that gun pointed right at her head."

Hawk had to work very hard to filter through all that information and not picture Anna with a gun to her head. Not think about the very real possibility Anna would say something rash and smart that would make him laugh like a loon.

And get her killed.

Palmer pulled his phone from his pocket. He showed Hawk the screen. "Mary is calling me."

"Go outside and take it. Don't tell her we're out here. Just get all the information you can from her."

Palmer nodded and then hurried outside. Hawk stayed where he was and listened to what was going on in the house. He could hear the low murmur of voices far off, but nothing more. He began to creep forward. Down the hall, as quietly as he could. He forced himself to be slow, methodical, even as he was desperate to run in guns blazing.

But that could get everyone killed, and the only thing that mattered was getting Anna out of this alive.

Alive, alive, alive. He repeated it to himself as he moved with slow, methodical purpose. A mantra. Speaking to any spiritual *whatever* his mother had believed in that would listen.

When Palmer rejoined him, Hawk had only moved maybe a quarter of the way down the hall.

"He's working alone, as far as anyone can tell," Palmer whispered. "Biggest hurdle is he hasn't stopped pointing the gun at Anna's head the whole time. He wants me to come in there. Once we're all there, he's going to kill Anna."

No. Hawk wasn't about to let that happen. He needed a plan and quick.

"Go around the house," he said to Palmer in a low whisper. "Go in from the dining room, but don't go into the living room. You step in, he could just pull that trigger, so you need to be quiet and stay out of sight. I'm going to make noise here. See if I can draw him out."

Palmer nodded.

"Shoot him. The minute I get him clear of Anna, you shoot. Even if I'm in the way."

"Hawk—"

"I mean it. She's number one. I'm collateral damage."

"You think she'd see it that way?"

They didn't have time for this argument, even whispered. "If she's alive, I don't give a damn how she sees it. Now go."

Palmer seemed to consider this and then nodded. "Give me three minutes to get around to that side of the house. Then I'll be ready for whatever happens."

It was Hawk's turn to nod. He watched Palmer go, started the countdown and crept closer to the living room, gun drawn and ready.

He'd save Anna and his baby no matter what it took.

Chapter Twenty-One

Anna was not good at waiting under any circumstances, but the whole gun-to-her-head thing was not making it any easier to keep her mouth shut and just *wait*.

Jack and Cash seemed like they could wait forever. Stoic walls of disapproval, though Anna knew them well enough to see the fury and worry simmering underneath. Mary had that bland expression on her face, but her eyes gave her away. Worry and terror. And Anna could hear Izzy crying behind Mary, though clearly the girl was trying to hold it together.

Anna's heart ached. This was too much for all of them, but definitely more than too much for an eleven-year-old.

The man with the gun, Darrin, was silent and patient. Way more patient than Anna. "Are we really just going to stand here all day waiting for my brother to show up?"

"I could knock you out again, and *then* kill you. Would you prefer that?" Darrin asked mildly.

Anna didn't bother to respond. She just sighed heavily and shifted on her feet. They were killing her. She was hungry, tired and thirsty. She wanted to cry and she wanted to rage.

She really wanted to punch this Darrin guy right in the face. She considered the angles. If she got an elbow up quickly enough, would it dislodge the gun or at least angle it away from her head?

The problem was, any stray bullet could hit any of the people she loved who were all across from them. Was there a way to angle her elbow backward so the gun went that way?

She considered all this, even though she'd considered it a million times. There had to be a way because she didn't think Palmer was coming. He was somewhere on the property, and obviously Mary had told the gunman he was coming, but Palmer had to know what had happened. He'd been outside with her. He'd likely followed her.

If he showed up, she'd be dead and they all knew it. So he very much shouldn't come. Gruesome death or no.

She didn't allow herself to think about Hawk. Maybe he was out there with Palmer. Maybe he was out at his office in Bent, completely unaware what was happening. It didn't matter where he was, as long as he was safe.

"This is taking too long," Darrin said. "I want him here. Now."

"We haven't invented teleportation, bud," Anna muttered.

He yanked her hair so hard she saw stars. Then he kicked out her legs so she fell to her knees. Hard enough she let out a pained hiss, barely managing to suppress a yelp.

"I've had enough of you," he said, shaking the hand that was fisted in her hair as she knelt there trying not to sob in pain.

Jack and Cash had moved forward, but that only prompted Darrin to shove the gun at the back of her head now. "I will shoot you all. I will kill every last one of you. I'd prefer it to end in emotional agony, but if it's your deaths, it'll be your deaths. You took my son away from me."

"Your son ran away from you," Jack returned. Coldly. "For whatever reasons, we had nothing to do with that or his death. We are sorry for your loss. We know—"

"Shut up!" Darrin screamed.

Anna tried not to wince at all the pain coursing through her. The bite of metal, the burning pain of him yanking her head around by the hair. She just had to breathe and be calm. She just had to survive.

She *had* to.

There was no way she could get away from Darrin's grasp right now, but she wasn't that far away from the guns her brothers had kicked over. She couldn't reach for one, but if she could get her leg out from under her without Darrin paying her any attention, maybe she could pull one toward her.

She shifted her weight, whimpering in pain. She *was* in pain, but the whimpering was put on.

"Stop squirming," Darrin ordered, pulling her hair again.

Her gasp of pain was real this time. "I can't sit on my knees like this," Anna said, wriggling even though it hurt like hell. But she managed to get into a seated position, her legs spread out in front of her. Darrin still had a grip on her hair and a gun pointed at her head.

She couldn't tell where Darrin was looking, but if it was at her siblings, maybe she could move her leg enough to get the gun.

She looked over at Jack and Cash. Their gazes were firmly on Darrin. No doubt watching her would be too hard on them. And they were looking for ways to eliminate the threat.

But Mary was watching her. Anna tried to use her eyes to get a message across. She looked at Mary. Then the gun. Then Darrin. Over and over again.

"Mr. Monroe," Mary said in that prim hostess voice of hers. Clearly trying to hold Darrin's attention so Anna could try to reach the gun. "I know you're upset and rightfully so. You lost a son. You want someone to blame."

"*You* are to blame! If you'd found him sooner, he would have been alive."

Anna wished she knew anything about this case, but when Jack had first started HSS, Anna had been so infuriated he was keeping her out of it that she'd refused to have *anything* to do with it. Fifteen wasn't an easy age for anyone, let alone a girl who'd lost both parents and was being raised by her grumpy older brother.

"Your son made his choices, Mr. Monroe. That isn't on us," Jack said firmly. Maybe a little coldly. Even though Anna knew Jack took every failure too much to heart.

She inched her foot closer to the gun. Darrin's grip on her hair kept her from being able to move much farther. She wouldn't be able to get either gun to herself, but she could kick out. Maybe hit one of them. Maybe send it back toward her brothers.

But she'd have to time it perfectly. Have to somehow get Darrin to stop pointing his gun at her head, even if he still held on to her hair. Would that be enough time?

It would have to be. "You know, I don't think Palmer's coming," Anna announced. Her brothers whipped their gazes to her, as if she was insane. And, well, maybe they weren't wrong. But she just kept talking.

If there was anything she was good at, it was talking

herself into problems her brothers solved. Right? Why not lean into it?

"He shows up, he knows you'll kill me. So why would he come? You thought that one through, Darrin?"

He jerked her hair again, and she winced at the pain that shot through her body. But she didn't stop. She couldn't stop. She needed just a few seconds where that gun wasn't pointed at her head.

"Honestly, this plan is just ridiculous. You should have kept trying to kill me when I was alone. Needing an audience has just dragged everything out. For every second we stand around here *waiting*, there's another cop figuring it out. They could be surrounding the house by now."

"Jesus, Anna," Cash muttered.

"I don't care about cops. I don't care if they catch me. I care about your suffering."

"I'm not suffering. I'm just bored," Anna returned, heaving out a sigh that allowed her to move her foot that much closer to the gun without Darrin looking down. "Aren't you bored, Darrin? Let's get this show on the road."

"Shut up. Just…shut up," he yelled, shaking her harder and harder until she had to shut up or she'd just scream in pain.

"Just let her go," Jack said in that authoritarian cop voice. "HSS is my creation. Your son was my responsibility. If you found our results lacking, you're mad at me. You're blaming me. Focus your anger on *me*."

Anna groaned. Loudly. "Oh my God, Jack. Why do you always have to be the martyr? Do you really think you're *that* important?"

Jack straightened, frowned at her. "It's my responsibility. HSS was created because of *me*."

Anna didn't know if Jack was playing along or if this was a real argument, but it didn't really matter. "Mr. Oldest Brother always thinking everything is his responsibility. Well, we're adults, too, you know? HSS is *all* of ours."

"You weren't even involved in this case, Anna. You were fifteen years old. Let her go, Mr. Monroe."

"Yeah, do what Jack says. He thinks everyone has to," Anna said, sounding as aggrieved as she possibly could.

"I cannot believe you're arguing at a time like this," Mary scolded—and Anna knew for sure *she* was playing along. Since Darrin couldn't see Anna's face from where he stood behind her, Anna grinned at Mary.

"And I can't believe you're making it all about you, Anna," Cash added. He wasn't smiling at her; in fact, he was frowning with all that fatherly disapproval he used on Izzy. But she knew it wasn't disapproval over what he was actually saying, but that this was her ploy. "Typical baby-of-the-family behavior."

"Shut up!" Darrin screamed, clearly losing whatever tenuous grasp on control he had, thanks to the sibling bickering. Who knew that would someday come in handy? "Fine! That's what you want. I'll just kill her. I'll just kill all of you!" But Darrin made a small mistake in the anger and frustration Anna had led him to. He lifted the gun from Anna's head and pointed it at Jack. "And you'll be the only survivor to grieve."

But the gun not being pointed at her anymore meant that everyone else could move. She was held by her hair, but she managed to kick out, which sent a gun skittering toward Jack.

Jack caught the gun, but before he could pick it up off the ground, a gunshot rang out. And all hell broke loose.

HAWK WATCHED AS Anna baited the man. He wasn't sure which feeling was more prevalent: one of frustration that she was *baiting* the man with the gun to her head, or one of awe that it was working.

Only Anna Hudson would come up with this ploy, for good or for ill.

Darrin was getting more and more angry, and while that made the chances of Darrin shooting Anna all the more possible, it was also making his arms shake. So if he pulled the trigger, it might not be aimed perfectly at Anna's head.

Then the siblings all joined in. At first Hawk was so angry that they weren't taking this seriously, he almost stepped into the fray. But when he caught Anna's profile grinning at Mary he realized this was some kind of…trick.

What the hell was wrong with the Hudsons? And why did he want to laugh in the midst of all this? That they would use the most unbelievable of arguments to distract a gunman. It was *insane*.

But it was working. Darrin was getting more and more red-faced and shaky. Hawk couldn't let this go on. He had to act. He was about to make a noise, just so Darrin would whirl on him, but Darrin started screaming. Palmer appeared behind his brothers, but it was clear he couldn't get off a good shot that didn't risk Anna.

So it was up to Hawk.

Everything happened too fast as Darrin pointed his gun at Jack. Hawk seized the moment. He had to. He pulled the trigger and shot. Then swore because he'd been so worried about hitting Anna, he'd missed Darrin entirely. The bullet crashed through the damn window.

But it shocked the gunman enough to let go of Anna

and whirl, which allowed Hawk to get off another shot that landed.

Unfortunately, so did Darrin.

The explosion of pain was a surprise. Hawk knew all about pain, but he'd never been shot and he didn't know what this felt like. He tried to stay upright, tried to make sure he saw what happened to Darrin, to make sure Anna got away.

He saw the front door splinter open, cops rushing in.

Then his body couldn't seem to hold him up any longer. Worse than the blow to the head. Worse than that one time someone had tried to run him over with their car. Worse than everything he could think of—physically, anyway.

It was just overwhelming. A black cloud of horribleness and he couldn't seem to move. Or was he moving? Was he writhing in pain or as still as a corpse?

Was he a corpse?

He could only lie there and stare at the ceiling, wondering if he was still alive. He knew there was a commotion, but he couldn't seem to hear it. Couldn't seem to get his mouth to work. Was this death?

He'd watched his mother slip away. It wasn't like this. She'd made horrible breathing noises. Muttered about going home. She'd slipped away.

He felt like he was being ripped in half. No homecoming. Just blackness.

Then he saw Anna crouch over him. She was yelling at people. Crying. Everything about her looked wild and desperate.

But she was alive, and wasn't that all that mattered? He couldn't care less what happened to him, as long as she was okay. He wanted to reach for her, tell her it was all okay. Maybe he did. He wasn't sure.

She disappeared for a few seconds as strangers knelt over him. He was almost certain they were EMTs, and that they were working on him. Maybe they'd bring him back to life, since he was most assuredly dead.

Because it couldn't be *good* that he didn't feel anything they were doing to him. Then he was moving. Or being moved? None of it quite made sense, but Anna was back in his vision. Tears streaming down her face. She really was just the prettiest thing, but he didn't want her crying over him. How on earth had he gotten so lucky?

Probably just another tally in the whole being-dead column. Hawk Steele hadn't had luck a day in his life… except that he'd had the best mother. And then Anna.

Finally something pierced the hazy world that surrounded him, a sharp bolt of pain. And then Anna's voice.

"Don't you *dare* die on me, you absolute jerk." Anna, sharp and demanding, just like she should be.

"Love you too, Blondie," he said, or tried to. He didn't feel fully within his body, but he kept his gaze on Anna's hazel eyes as long as he could.

She was okay and that was all that mattered. Her and the baby. Okay. Taken care of.

Who needed him, anyway?

Chapter Twenty-Two

Anna was held back as the medics rolled Hawk away on a stretcher. She fought anyone who tried to hold her back, but there were too many people. Every person she managed to shove away, a new person came in to grab her.

Until she was finally met with the brick wall that was Grant. He looked right at her with dark eyes. Their father's eyes. "Stop," he said. Forcefully. Sharply. When everyone else had been pleading.

And she didn't know what else to do, so she stopped. Looked up at him and he pulled her into a tight hug, when out of all of them, Grant was the least likely to hug *anyone*. She'd barely even seen him hold Dahlia's hand.

But he held her there and all that spiraling panic stilled into just…straight-up fear. But Grant held her tight and spoke calmly and low in her ear.

"There is no point going in the ambulance. He'll have to go straight into the ER. Dahlia and I will drive you to the hospital so you can wait more comfortably."

"But—"

"No buts." He shifted her so he had his arm around her shoulders and started propelling her forward.

"But Pita…"

"Cash is handling the dogs. The EMTs cleared him

and Izzy to stay home and take it easy, and they stitched Mary up. Just a scratch—she doesn't even need to go in. Palmer and Louisa are going to stay here with them and keep an eye on things." Grant just kept leading her to his truck, where Dahlia stood waiting for them.

They ushered her into the back of the truck, and Dahlia climbed in next to her. She held Anna's hand the entire interminable ride to the hospital. They led her to the waiting room and didn't let her talk to anyone. They kept her in a bubble, in a cocoon.

But none of it mattered until someone told her...

Dahlia continued to hold Anna's hand, though she realized now it was less about comforting her and more about keeping her still while Grant talked to various hospital employees.

When Grant returned, it was with a doctor. Anna scowled at them both, but she didn't fight off the doctor as the woman checked her out. She sat still and miserable and let the woman examine her scalp and ask droning questions about how she felt.

Like my entire heart was ripped out, thanks a lot.

Eventually the doctor left. Anna didn't even bother to ask what the consensus was. She wasn't leaving this seat until someone was ready to let her see Hawk.

After a considerable amount of time, hours, days, she didn't know, someone came to stand in front of her. She could tell by the shoes it wasn't a doctor, so she didn't look up at first. She really didn't want to deal with anyone. No doubt her family or a cop, but she just...wanted to be alone in her own horrible thoughts to wallow in fear and awful things. In the bubble, in the cocoon where she could live in denial. Forever.

But when she forced herself to look up, it was Jack standing there. He looked rough. As rough as back when Mom and Dad had first disappeared. When he'd been left in charge of five kids and a mystery they still hadn't solved.

How did he stand it?

Without saying a word, Grant got up and let Jack take his seat. So Jack sat next to her, looked right at her, and there was a softness, a vulnerability there in his gaze she wasn't sure he'd ever allowed her to see before. "I'm sorry," he said, his voice rough.

At first she assumed it was just the thing to be said. *Sorry the man you love might be dead because you're such a horrible person.* But she realized this was Jack and that was a guilty "I'm sorry."

She stared at him. "You… You aren't honestly blaming yourself."

He took a sharp breath in. "I created HSS because I needed to *do* something. I should have considered that it might eventually put us in danger. And it has, over and over again, but never like this. You became a target because of a choice *I* made."

She stared at him for a good minute. Then she shook her head. "Jack, you are an honest-to-God fool."

He got that pinched look on his face she often brought out in him, but even if he didn't mean to, he made her realize something very important. "The only person's fault this is is the man who couldn't handle his son's death. And I can't imagine. Don't want to." Her hand rested on her belly, almost like a reflex. Like she could protect the little bundle of cells in there. "But his grief isn't our fault. His break with reality isn't our fault. His violence isn't our fault. Deep down, I hope you know that."

He didn't say anything to that, but that was how she knew he was trying to take it on board. That he wasn't arguing with her.

"I love you, and I've never thanked you for everything you've done for us. I've only ever given you a hard time. It's all I've ever been any good at."

"Well, I guess that saved our lives today, Annie."

She opened her mouth to argue, but then she just kind of…laughed. Maybe it had. But Hawk was still… She swallowed. Hard. "I don't know how to lose him, Jack. I barely had him."

Jack nodded, then took her hand. "He isn't gone yet."

A few minutes later a nurse came over. "Are any of you family of Hawk Steele?"

Anna stood. "I'm his fiancée." Because they were getting married. They were going to raise this baby together. And have more. Yes, they'd have more and be happy and build a house at the Hudson Ranch and…and… Everything would be okay.

It had to be.

HAWK FIGURED THIS strange black floaty area he was in had to be death. Hell, maybe. He probably deserved it. There was blackness and no pain and no escape. Just this weird nothing.

And then he heard something that was pain. Because he hadn't heard it in years.

His mother's voice. *Hawk.*

He tried to see through the black. See her face. Find her. His heart scrambled and none of it made sense, except his yearning to hear it again. To see her again. "Mom."

But it was just her voice, whispering around him. *Go on home, baby.*

"I don't have a home."

Sure you do.

And then it was gone. Her voice. Any sense he'd had of her in this black world of nothingness. But then he heard…Anna's voice. Felt something squeeze his hand, and he knew it was her.

His home.

He blinked his eyes open and was met with hazel ones. The ones he'd met across the smoky barroom and felt something. Immediately. The moment their gazes had locked.

He opened his mouth, but whatever came out wasn't words.

"Shh. Give yourself time," she said, brushing a kiss across his hand in hers. Things went black. Then she was there again. He was in and out. Then he dozed off. Then he woke up.

He wasn't sure how long it took, but eventually he was awake and with it enough to remember what had happened, to understand where he was and how to talk again.

He supposed he hadn't *really* heard his mother's voice. It had been a dream or something. But he also knew of all the spiritual things his mother had believed, him hearing her voice would have been one of them.

He turned his head. Anna was still there, though she'd dozed off in the chair she'd pulled next to his bed. She was holding his hand limply. She was pale and no doubt needed a good meal and some good sleep.

"Blondie."

She jumped straight to alertness at impressive speed. "You're awake. You're talking."

"Yeah. I guess I'm going to live, huh?"

She leaned forward, studying every inch of him. "That's what they say. I guess the only worry now is infection."

And clearly she *was* worried, because she just sat there staring at him, holding his hand like it was her only lifeline.

And if he wasn't mistaken, guilt lurking deep in those hazel eyes.

"You know as well as I do, someone was going to get shot in that scenario. I'd rather it be me than you. A hundred times over."

She swallowed. "Doesn't mean I have to like it," she croaked.

He could tell she was close to tears, but he didn't want that. He wanted this to be...positive. Moving toward happy. "Besides, now you owe me one. You can pay me back. In the bedroom. Once I'm up for that sort of thing again. So, like, tomorrow."

She rolled her eyes. "In your dreams."

He tried to pull her hand up to his mouth but couldn't quite make it. He sighed. "What about this Darrin guy?"

"Arrested. Hart isn't sure he'll be considered fit to stand trial. But he'll get help if he isn't, so that's something. Tripp, the ranch hand, he's in a coma, I guess. Chessa's... missing. No one's sure if she's dead or alive. They'll keep looking for her, though."

Hawk nodded but felt tired again. Worn to the bone, and like he'd doze off again. "You should go home. Get some real rest."

"Like I could rest with you in here. I'm not going anywhere for the duration. So, you want me to rest, you're going to have to recover fast."

He didn't know whether he was amused or resigned, he was so tired. "I'll see what I can do."

"Hawk."

His eyes had closed on him, but he managed to open them again and look at her. She was very grim and serious.

"The minute you can stand for more than five minutes at a time, we're going down to the courthouse and getting married."

"Thought you wanted a real wedding."

"I don't care anymore. I just want to be married."

He saw all the pain and worry in her eyes. And he wanted to give her everything. Because she'd given him everything. Love, a family. Home. "I'm going to have to insist on a white dress. Your family. And a honeymoon."

"I'll do whatever you want," she said, so solemnly. So seriously.

He looked at her and laughed. Maybe it was the painkillers. Maybe it was just knowing her. "No, you won't. And thank God for that."

Her mouth curved. "Well, I'll try for a little while, anyway."

"Okay, maybe we should take a bet on how long that lasts." Pain was slithering through the cloud of weird exhaustion, and he tried to find a comfortable position.

She snorted, but then she stood and leaned over him. She brushed his hair off his forehead, in a move that poignantly reminded him of his mother. And he remembered the blackness.

"I heard my mom's voice," he heard himself say, though he hadn't thought he'd meant to tell her that. Surely it sounded way too out there.

Anna stilled and tears filled her eyes. "What did she say?"

"She told me to go home."

"Not, like, heavenly home, I hope."

"No." He looked up at her. Anna had changed the course of his life. And thank God, because whatever came next with her—marriage, kids, a *life*—it was better than anything he'd planned or hoped for. "No, I think she meant you."

A tear fell over onto her cheek, then dripped down onto his. Anna wiped it away, then leaned down and pressed her mouth to his. "I love you," she murmured.

"I love you, too."

And when they got married a few weeks later, she wore a white dress and Pita wore a bow tie. All her family was there, and they did it at the ranch, rather than a courthouse. Izzy was the flower girl, and there were quite a few canine guests.

And as they repeated their "I dos," a hawk swooped down and perched on the eaves of the house, as if looking down at them. Anna squeezed his hand and grinned at him, because as much as he resisted all the woo-woo stuff his mother had loved, Anna had leaned into it, and was now constantly talking to him about spirit guides and ghosts and all that other nonsense.

Which didn't feel so much like nonsense in the moment. So, with what felt like his mother watching, he promised himself to Anna and his baby.

Because Hawk Steele considered himself a man who rolled with the punches—and Anna Hudson, now Anna Hudson-Steele, and their baby-to-be was the best sucker punch he'd ever get.

* * * * *